M000286472

Casablanca AND OTHER STORIES

Casablanca

AND OTHER STORIES

Edgar Brau

Translated from the Spanish by
Andrea G. Labinger, Joanne M. Yates,
and Donald A. Yates

Introduction by Donald A. Yates

Michigan State University Press

East Lansing

CASS DISTRICT LIBRARY
319 MICHIGAN RD 62N
CASSOPOLIS MI 49031

Copyright © 2006 by Andrea G. Labinger, Joanne M. Yates, and Donald A. Yates

Assistance in the preparation of this book has been provided by a generous translation grant administered by the National Endowment for the Arts.

NATIONAL
ENDOWMENT
FOR THE ARTS

Published by arrangement with Julie Popkin, Literary Agent, 15340 Albright Street #204, Pacific Palisades, California 90272.

♾ The paper used in this publication meets the minimum requirements of ANSI/NISO Z39.48-1992 (R 1997) (Permanence of Paper).

Michigan State University Press
East Lansing, Michigan 48823-5245

Printed and bound in the United States of America.

11   10   09   08   07   06   1   2   3   4   5   6   7   8   9   10

LIBRARY OF CONGRESS CATALOGING-IN-PUBLICATION DATA

Brau, Edgar, 1958–
    [Short stories. English. Selections]
    Casablanca and other stories / by Edgar Brau ; translated from the Spanish
by Andrea G. Labinger, Joanne M. Yates, and Donald A. Yates.
      p. cm.
    ISBN-13: 978-0-87013-768-6 (casebound : alk. paper)
    ISBN-10: 0-87013-768-9 (casebound : alk. paper)
    1. Brau, Edgar, 1958—Translations into English. I. Labinger, Andrea G.
II. Title.
    PQ7798.12.R346A2 2006
    863'.64–dc22

                          2006017109

Cover and book design by Erin Kirk New

Michigan State University Press is a member of the Green Press Initiative and is committed to developing and encouraging ecologically responsible publishing practices. For more information about the Green Press Initiative and the use of recycled paper in book publishing, please visit www.greenpressinitiative.org.

Visit Michigan State University Press on the World Wide Web at:
www.msupress.msu.edu

963.64
RRA

CONTENTS

ACKNOWLEDGMENTS

The translators wish to acknowledge the first appearance in English of the following stories in the publications indicated:

"The Journey" and "Bárcena's Dog" in *Two Lines*
"The Siesta" in *Ellery Queen Mystery Magazine*
"The Forgotten God" in *The Antioch Review*
"The Prisoner" in *The Literary Review*
"The Blessing" in *Beacons 2003*
"The Calendar" in *Source*
"The Poem" in *Nimrod*

The stories included here were originally published in Spanish in the following volumes:

"Casablanca" in *Casablanca* (Buenos Aires: Metzengerstein, 2003)
"The Journey," "The Forgotten God," "The Prisoner," "The Blessing,"
    "The Calendar," "The Buddha's Eyes," and "The Poem" in *El Poema y
    otras historias* (Buenos Aires: Antigua Librería de Marie Roget, 1992)
"The Siesta" and "Bárcena's Dog" in *Tres cuentos* (Buenos Aires:
    Metzengerstein, 1998)

INTRODUCTION

Edgar Brau, who was born in 1958 in Resistencia in the northern Argentine province of Chaco, turned to writing only after pursuing a number of other possible careers. He spent his early years fishing, exploring the Chaqueño jungle and, more than anything else, reading. At the age of ten he moved with his family to Buenos Aires. After five years he withdrew from formal schooling, continued reading voraciously and indulged his passions for soccer, rugby, and boxing. But for a chronic respiratory problem, he might well have pursued a career as a boxer. In his eighteenth year he was drawn to the theater, where he began performing as an actor. Between 1976 and 1986 he broadened his interests to include directing and staging, and during this period presented works by Molière, Labiche, Claudel, Chekhov, and Shakespeare.

In 1986 he won the first prize in a short story competition sponsored by the Italian embassy in Buenos Aires, and thereafter he concentrated his creative energies on writing. His first volume of short stories, *El Poema y otras historias,* was published in 1992. At that moment Brau decided that he would have to support his literary career with a practical sideline, so he opened a bookshop. (To offer a comment on Brau's capacities as a businessman, I have noted during visits to his small shop on Paraná Street in Buenos Aires that it is not easy to buy a book from him. Generous and courteous to a fault, he prefers to give them away. Once, when I invited him to have a cup of coffee at a *confitería* around the corner, I asked if it would be convenient for him to close the shop briefly. He replied with a wry smile that the economic benefit to him—whether the store was open or closed—was about the same. I see him as the somewhat impractical but consummate artist.)

His first novel, *El comediante,* was published in 1995, and, as was the case with his short story collection, it received a most encouraging, if limited, critical reception. From his earliest years as an author, Brau has been reluctant to promote the merits of his writings. He has never cultivated the literary society of Buenos Aires and has shunned the very visible circuit of cocktail parties and book presentations. Nor has he attempted to have his books given wide circulation among literary critics in the hope of securing exploitable critical opinions. In a letter to me he explained why he has chosen not to get involved in the business of self-promotion: "In Buenos Aires," he wrote, "nobody will refuse you a cigarette or a flattering book review."

In this regard, I sense that Brau is following the model of the late Argentine writer, Marco Denevi (1922–1998), who also distanced himself from the social, convivial, and commercial aspects of something that he thought was very serious and very personal—literature. Denevi's stature as a writer was, nonetheless, firmly established at the time of his death.

I read Brau's first collection of short stories some months before making a trip to Argentina and ran into him, coincidentally, when I visited his bookshop in the capital. He gave me a warm welcome when I introduced myself, saying that he remembered that I had collaborated in bringing out in 1962 a book titled *Labyrinths*, the first volume of the fiction and essays of Brau's compatriot, Jorge Luis Borges, in English translation.

I told Brau that I had been particularly impressed by the literary style that he, a completely unheralded Argentine author, had demonstrated in "El Poema," the title story of that first book. It was a sincere homage to Borges that evoked both Borgesian themes and tone. I pointed out, too, that his boundless imagination and versatility were clearly evident in all the stories included in his first collection. With his unhesitating approval, I decided it was time to see if Brau's stories could be brought into English.

The present collection includes seven of the ten stories from *El Poema y otras historias*, together with two of the three narratives that were included in his 1998 *Tres cuentos*.

As these stories began appearing in translation in U.S. magazines, Brau began to attract attention. In 2003 he was invited to spend two semesters on the faculty at the University of Nevada–Reno as Writer in Residence. It was there that he wrote "Casablanca," which leads off this first volume of his work in translation. That story is the single most memorable indication to date of his maturing literary talent.

The presence of scenes of Argentine life in his writing is almost a constant, but it is natural in him also to cultivate a vein of fantasy. It is easy at times to be reminded of Poe in his pages. This influence is something that Brau will not deny. There seems to be, in fact, a kind of affinity between the two writers. "The Buddha's Eyes" may well strike the reader as notably Poesque. And there is a curious reverberation in the two names: Edgar Allan Poe and Edgar Aldo Brau.

The theme of torture is prominent in Brau's work. In "Bárcena's Dog" he finds a nineteenth-century historical precedent that foreshadows events of the tragic years of the "dirty war" that was waged in Argentina in the 1970s. This more recent period serves as a background for the unsettling events of his story titled "The Prisoner." Focusing on this same contemporary period, in 2000 Brau published *Suite argentina,* which is a set of four narratives all of which deal with grim aspects of the capture and torture of suspected subversives by the Argentine military government.

In "The Siesta" Brau offers a tale of perfect irony, where torture of a different sort is an indirect motivating factor. With "The Calendar" an element of fantasy is delicately introduced into a realistic setting. And "The Journey" is totally fanciful and impressionistic. Brau reveals a satirical side in "The Blessing," a story that the late Marco Denevi might have been pleased to write.

In "The Forgotten God," the author's freewheeling imagination allows him to attempt to depict what could be considered as something ineffable. Here, incidentally, he undertakes what Borges succeeded in doing so brilliantly—fashioning literature from literature.

Argentine writers have made many important contributions to the emergence of Latin American literature and its incorporation in our time "into the mainstream" of western culture, as critic Luis Harss has proposed. Edgar Brau, I believe, can justifiably be included in the ranks of those whose work today merits the attention of readers of the widest possible audience.

Donald A. Yates

❧ Casablanca

It happened toward the end of March, on the road to Mar del Plata. At the close of a very warm day, the sun was slowly setting. In the western sky, a blend of pinks and grays distracted me from the solitary route and the storm advancing from the south. When the sun was swallowed by the horizon, followed by that inevitable, final burst of silence, I turned my attention once more to the road in front of me. Intensified by the darkness, the road plunged into the threatening, vaporous hollow of the storm, which a convulsive movement seemed to push closer, its foremost section already ahead of me. Alongside the road, the swaying green of the trees and shrubs was rapidly turning black, and a murky wind propelled flocks of birds forward. I slowed down a bit and glanced at my watch: a few minutes before eight. I had figured on reaching the coast by ten. But now I had to move very slowly; a pale blue haze, as swift as the storm, impeded my progress. I advanced a few hundred yards very gradually, fascinated by the silken wall, a perfect reflection—or detached piece—of the squall that was developing up above, feeling all the while as though I were traveling through a movie set. I considered the possibility of accelerating and plunging right into it, of passing through it as in a magic act. A lightning bolt crashing into a cluster of eucalyptus trees and two or three raindrops bursting against my windshield made me abandon that notion. I shifted into reverse, looking for a turnoff I had seen a few miles back, next to a billboard advertising a brand of coffee. I felt the storm pursuing me. But a side road leading west that I hadn't noticed before caught my attention before I reached the turnoff. On a sign placed almost at ground level, an arrow pointed the way; beneath the arrow, barely discernible through the rust, appeared the word *Casablanca*.

I made the turn; the commotion of wind and clouds compelled me to find refuge. In the north, increasingly dim, the last clear outline of horizon disappeared. I advanced with my headlights on along a gravel path bordered by tall trees. After about two miles, a tight curve once more turned me toward the south, facing a door whose brick columns stood partially in ruins. A tin cutout hung from one of the columns (in spite of the layers of rust and the faded colors, I was able to identify it as the image of something like a Moorish guard). In the middle of the arch that connected both columns, held in place by a couple of pieces of wire, dangled a sign whose letters repeated the word *Casablanca.*

At the end of the path (now there were trees only along the edge closest to the road; on the other side, just the empty prairie), a cluster of buildings hazily emerged from clouds of dust and leaves.

As I passed through the gate, an initial torrent of rain obliterated the path. I advanced blindly a few more yards, watching for the momentary breaks produced whenever the wind changed the direction of the rain or whenever the rain let up briefly. I leaned forward, pressing my forehead to the windshield. After a couple of minutes, a few flashes of lightning clearly defined the details of a house; I could also see a boy leaning against the wall beneath the porch cover, observing me. I cut the motor and started to get out, but the rain resumed with more intensity. To my right, the darkness was impenetrable; to the left was the fuzzy outline of some sort of shed. Suddenly the rain abated, and at that point, the boy ran toward the shed. I opened the car door and could see that it was actually quite a sophisticated structure—or at least an unusual one for a place like that. It was probably about thirty-five feet long, and it was gray; in the middle, framed by two wooden rectangles with small, raised rings, was an iron double door in a darker shade of gray, with triangular moldings. Above the door was a sign with white fluorescent letters that, like the broken garland surrounding it, was unlit, and, rising from some weed-filled stone blocks on either side, a large white arch enclosed the whole thing.

I got out of the car, and, urged on by a gust of wind and water, ran to the half-opened door (I managed to read the word *Rick* or something like that on the sign). A very dim light blinked from inside. I pushed open the door, unsurprised by the squeaking hinges; even in my rush to get out of the rain, I'd noticed that the place looked practically abandoned. I walked in, but a stack of tables and chairs blocked my way; the light came from a kerosene lantern by the entrance. Without taking another step, I clapped my hands, shouting out a greeting. At first there was silence, and then I began to hear the sound of a piano. I recognized the tune immediately: it was the theme song from the film *Casablanca*. Soon it was accompanied by the voice of the black man who sang it in the movie (despite the clarity of the sound, I imagined it must be something like a gramophone with its heavy, metal disk). Then, skirting around the tables and chairs, I found myself staring at a wide, deep room with white walls and arches, its central corridor surrounded by tables with lamps on top. The tables, chairs, and tablecloths all were in lighter or darker shades of gray; the lamps (fringes dangled from the lampshades) were white. The music came from the rear left, and it obviously wasn't a record; seated at a piano, a black man played and sang the famous song perfectly—a perfect imitation, that is. Next to him, standing alongside a solitary cymbal from a percussion set, was the boy I had seen running. The man, in profile, performed the piece as if no one else were there; the boy stared at me suspiciously. I inched forward very slowly, impeded by a sense of unreality. The place smelled like burned kerosene and tobacco, and the sound of rain against the metal roof resounded from somewhere. Crystal chandeliers hung from the ceiling, but none of them was lit; the irregular light, flickering in the air currents, was provided by a few kerosene lanterns and some candles distributed throughout the room, always next to a mirror. Most of the upholstered chairs were threadbare, the floor tiles cracked; in the vases, silk flowers, perhaps charming once in an artificial way, now looked more like dried flowers that steeped the walls in gloom, the silhouette of their heads bobbing laboriously up and down in the flickering light like Chinese shadow puppets. In the center of the room, to my right, its (black and white) chips scattered as though by a child, was a roulette table, completely gray. I felt—as I took in and registered those props with astonishment—that even though everything in the place fit perfectly, the hint of silence behind the incidental music, the unoccupied chairs, the absence of those for whom each detail had been arranged, rendered them curiously incompatible: a warehouse full of antiques whose merchandise had been organized by a man in a blindfold.

I walked up to the piano player without feeling obliged to stop: his concentration on singing and playing was complete—only the boy kept following me with his gaze. By the wall opposite the piano, a man in dark glasses (his face seemed familiar at first glance), a white jacket and black bow tie dozed, his chin resting on his chest. He was sitting at a table with a screen behind it; on the table there was a chess set, a full ashtray, and an ordinary drinking glass, now empty. In another chair lay an untidy pile of a dozen or so books. The bar, which occupied the entire rear section, stopped me in my tracks. Entirely gray and white, it was a semicircle bordered with smaller semicircles at both ends; farther back, a large mirror, soiled by dust and time, separated the shelves, which were lined with empty bottles; practically none of the round barstools was in good shape. At one end of the bar, almost directly parallel to the piano, a winding staircase led to the upper floor. Even without music, I thought, it was possible to recognize the set from *Casablanca*. Impressed by that display, I even imagined the very unlikely possibility that it had been filmed there; after all, stranger things have happened in our country. And yet, that replica of a black-and-white photo and that black man, playing an upright piano just like the one in the movie . . . I leaned against one of the barstools and turned toward the center of the room in order to get a complete picture. Condensed within that gray, dead tableau beneath that roof, all the years that had passed since the movie was made suddenly seemed to hang over my head, suffocating me. I stepped away, feeling faint, and turned again toward the bar, and, as though it were a vision in a dream, I stared at myself in the mirror for what now seems to have been a very long moment. Another reflection joined mine, and immediately a voice saved me.

"Good evening, sir. Sir?"

I turned around. It was the piano player. He had finished his song and was now standing, his hands folded over at his waist. The boy had disappeared.

"Good evening, sir," he repeated when I turned around to look at him, and then, nodding his head slightly, he inquired, "Alone?"

"Yes. Good evening. The rain . . . I . . . ," I replied, cutting my answer short with astonishment as I noted his resemblance to Sam, the black piano player in the movie. In fact, he was identical, although much older; his hair was completely white, and his belly kept his suit jacket unbuttoned—it was gray satin, just like in the film, only quite shabby and darned in more than one place.

"Welcome to Casablanca," he added, pointing to the room with a broad gesture, like a master of ceremonies. His voice sounded hoarse and some-what disappointed now.

I glanced around the room, as did he, very soberly. Then, regaining his composure, he added, "Welcome to Rick's American Café," indicating, like an announcer, the man who was dozing at the table and whom I had until now taken for a waiter.

I took a few steps forward; the piano player's allusion confirmed (explained) the other man's familiar appearance: he reminded me of Bogart in *Casablanca*. I leaned over to see him better, and the other man laughed.

"Yes, sir, that's Rick," he corroborated with a certain pride when I turned toward him again. "A pretty old Rick, for sure, and a sickly one. The years, sir, who can escape them?"

I stood up, and the pianist violently stuck a chord. The man in glasses awoke with a start, then tilted his head to one side, listening. I shivered; in full face, even with glasses, he looked just like Humphrey Bogart. An eighty-something-year-old Bogart, with a bad dye job and plenty of wrinkles.

"Sam?" he asked gently, leaning forward.

The black man smiled at me, as pleased as if a pet had responded to his command to be exhibited to a visitor. Then he played a few strident bars on the piano, went over to the other man, and said, "Yes, Rick, I'm here. And we have a guest. But he's not a tourist. It's raining hard out there."

The man turned his head in various directions, trying to find me. I greeted him, but the piano player motioned me not to come any closer.

"Good evening," I repeated, drawing closer to the table.

The man responded with a nearly imperceptible nod of his head; then he adjusted his position, ran his hand through his hair, and rummaged in his pocket. He pulled out a half-smoked cigarette and lit it with a match. He took a few drags, grabbed the glass with his other hand, searching for the black man with his gaze (I noticed his movements were no longer so natural). The piano player had stepped behind the bar; he bent down for a second, reappearing with two glasses and a partially consumed bottle of cheap gin. The other man waited, partly afflicted and partly resigned, behind the cigarette smoke. When the piano player served him the gin, he took a sip, removed his glasses (his eyes looked normal and were watery, like Bogart's), gripped the glass with both hands and stared off at a fixed point in the distance with the same tormented expression the actor used to have. Immediately, the piano player handed me a glass of gin, showing me to a table by the piano, where we sat down.

"To what once was our Casablanca," he said, raising his glass to clink it against mine. "And Rick's Café," he added, in a somewhat melancholy tone (which struck me as an affectation) and took a swig.

I waited a few seconds, about to ask what it all meant, but the other man interrupted.

"Ilsa, Ilsa," he said, biting off the words and hanging his head, defeated; the cigarette fell to the floor. Then he rubbed his face violently, said a few words in English that I didn't really understand, took another swig, put on his eyeglasses, and in a different, casual voice (as though neither the question nor my answer mattered very much), asked, "Where you from, *mister?*"

"Buenos Aires," I replied, raising my voice.

"Everyone's from Buenos Aires," he remarked in the same neutral voice, twisting his mouth to one side.

The black man smiled wearily, still looking at me. I interpreted his silence as a way of telling me I should respond.

"And you?" I asked, just to ask something.

"Take a guess," he challenged, removing his eyeglasses and offering me a crooked smile.

The name Humphrey Bogart flashed predictably through my mind.

"North America," I answered without thinking.

The man laughed, with the famous actor's measured laughter. The piano player joined in, and so did I, in my case because I didn't understand what they were laughing about.

"Why North American?" the man persisted after another drink. The black man gave me a crafty look that I didn't quite comprehend.

"Your face . . . and because you speak English," I explained, all the while imagining how weak my explanation must have sounded.

The man stepped back with a sarcastic smile on his lips, raising his hand a few times as though weighing something. Then he reacted.

"But *mister,*" he said, putting on his eyeglasses again, "*je ne parle pas anglais; yo no hablo inglés.* I speak French and Spanish." And mockingly, in the same voice he had used to pronounce the English word *mister* (Bogart's voice), he continued, "Tell me, how can you imagine I would even attempt to pronounce that salad of consonants some ancient Saxon tossed together at the edge of a swamp while he gathered acorns to eat? English? Please! That language is just a bunch of acorns rattling around in a leather bag. Believe me, *mister,* it's a nutshell between the teeth of a crazy squirrel."

I looked at the books piled up on the chair.

"Shakespeare was no acorn," I taunted, leaning toward his table with my eyes on the piano player, who seemed to be enjoying this.

"Bah," he snorted. "Shakespeare, Shakespeare. An acorn for exportation, *mister.* Listen: people should read him in French, like I do. You still get the idea, and at least the container is civilized. Read him in Spanish, if you like, or in Italian, you see my point. But Shakespeare in English? Bah!"

And he leaned forward to get my reaction.

The black man and I smiled silently. Then, unsure of the effect his speech had produced, he added, *"Play it again, Sam.* Tell me, don't you think that sounds like someone spitting out a wad of tobacco?"

This time we laughed out loud, although my laughter wasn't as natural as it might have been; *that face, just like Bogart's,* talking about all those things, and in that place, brought back the feeling of unreality I had experienced a moment before, the uneasiness that assails us sometimes in dreams, or when we realize we've been dreaming. Meanwhile, the black man had gone off for more gin. The man stepped away, satisfied (he reminded me of a puppy getting a treat) and immediately asked Sam to bring him the books.

"Please, Sam, my Racine, my Baudelaire, my Balzac, my Flaubert, my Valéry, my Proust," he said jokingly, as if trying to show me the quality of his reading material, while the piano player gathered up the volumes.

Sam placed the books next to the chess set and before withdrawing, whispered something in his ear; the man nodded slightly.

Then Sam went over to the piano and returned to our table with a portrait I hadn't noticed before. The other man had removed his eyeglasses and began leafing through some of the books.

"He can't read them now; Fortunato, my godson, reads them to him. It's gobbledy-gook, of course, because he doesn't know French, and all the books are in that language. But it's okay because he knows them all by heart," the piano player confided, leaning toward me with the portrait between his knees. "And that business about English is an old story; he speaks it just fine and he likes it, but he says those things because of an Englishwoman who left him many years ago and whom he can't forgive. Rick is Argentine, from Córdoba, but as a boy he moved to Buenos Aires, to the capital. There, he . . ." he stopped, as if he had been about to commit an act of disloyalty or betray a confidence whose moment hadn't arrived. He took a sip of his gin and balanced the portrait on the table, turning it toward me. "The owner of Casablanca," he announced by way of explanation, serving a bit more gin.

In the photograph was the actor who plays Ferrari in the movie, the owner of that café or whatever it was called, the Blue Parrot, the guy Ilsa and Victor go to see to try to get a safe-conduct. His head was covered by a fez and his eyes were smiling.

"Ah, yes, Greenstreet, the one who plays Ferrari," I remarked confidently.

"It seems you know the movie quite well," Sam said, looking at me with interest.

"I've seen it four or five times. The last time was about three months ago."

The black man smiled, shifted the portrait a little more in my direction, and replied, "But this time you're mistaken, sir. This man in the photo isn't . . . the actor you said. It's Señor Ferrari, of course, but that's just what we call him because he looks a lot like the man in the movie and because he likes us to call him that. Señor Ferrari isn't an actor; he was a ranch owner and he started this place."

I took the portrait and looked at it more carefully. In effect, the resemblance to the actor was also remarkable in this case, but not as perfect as with the other two: Greenstreet was perhaps a bit younger and thinner. I placed it back on the table, allowing Sam to continue. I understood that I no longer needed to ask about this place or its meaning; he was there to be my guide.

"Like I was telling you, this place was . . . is Casablanca. And this is Rick's Café, like in the movie. Nothing is missing, you can see. Well, it's not the same anymore, but as long as some of us are still here, it'll keep on being Rick's Café. The café . . ."

A lightning bolt made him stop. The noise of the rain against the tin roof grew stronger. He took another sip of gin and, turning momentarily toward the back of the room, remarked, "Looks like it's going to rain for a while." Then, looking me quickly up and down, he continued, "Luckily we have this place to help people. If not for us, what would become of folks who travel this road?"

I caught his meaning: everything was going to be more expensive here than elsewhere. But in order to leave him guessing, I nodded very slightly and began observing the phony Rick, who had an open book practically against his face and was reading—or pretending to read—a page. At the same time, the piano player didn't take his eyes off me. When I turned back to him again, he sat down in the chair and continued talking.

"Rick's Café; Rick's *American* Café," he said in a dreamy voice, staring at the entryway. "Right there, where you entered, I entered, too, exactly fifty-two years ago, in January of 1950, the first week of January, to be exact. I was twenty-five years old and I had just arrived in Buenos Aires from Uruguay. Señor Ferrari discovered me in the doorway of the hotel on Avenida de Mayo where I was a bellhop and he hired me (I remember how he yelled 'Sam!' when he passed by on the sidewalk and saw me). Yes, sir, I signed a contract and everything, and I was going to earn ten times what I was earning at the hotel. Everything was almost ready here for the performances. Almost all the others were here already, even me—" he interrupted himself, smiling. "Sam, I mean, the man who was going to play Sam until then, a Brazilian faggot who played the piano in a bar in El Bajo, in Buenos Aires, where the women stripped. But Señor Ferrari picked me, even though I wasn't old enough. He was going to have to put makeup on me, he said after he fired the other guy. In those days, I already had a hoarse voice and I knew how to carry a tune (I learned at Carnival in Uruguay), and I could also manage pretty well on the piano. My mother was a maid, and when I was a kid I used to go with her to this family that had a piano; I learned a little bit there and later in a hotel in Montevideo where I started working when I was fifteen—the piano player in the salon at the hotel used to let me practice when there were no customers around. But even that wasn't enough to play Sam. Señor Ferrari brought in a professor who made me practice all day long for about two months. The professor was strict and he wouldn't even let me go out to eat, but the day of the premiere everyone thought I was the piano player from the film; I had to speak Spanish to convince them otherwise. And then Señor Ferrari paid me double and even introduced me to a blonde, a little older than me, who was from Mar del Plata where she was spending the summer and who had had too much to drink. I couldn't leave the place without permission, so that's how I had my very first white woman, inside a car, in a eucalyptus grove right around here. But the truth is that everyone was great that night, why would I lie to you? Rick, Elsa, Ugarte, Strasser, Renault, Victor Laszlo, the orchestra, everyone was very good—even Señor Ferrari, who played Ferrari but hadn't practiced much."

He stopped to rub his eyes. I looked at the room and everything suddenly seemed to come to life. (My memory had inserted a scene from the film with its noise and movement.) He waited, then continued with his tale.

"Now you look at this empty place and you must think it was always like this. Lots of people do. But, sir, this was just like in the movie. I always say the same thing to people who come in here and they think they're dreaming, or else they think we've gone crazy; there was the movie, and there was this café. The movie was a fake, but in *our* Casablanca, everything was real. I remember how Señor Ferrari always used tell his friends that he let them *into* the movie, that here they could touch things they could only see in the movie. That's why I think we were so successful. Even General Perón came here once, the year after we opened. He was a shrewd one; he took Elsa to the Presidential summer resort for a few days, out in Chapadmalal. At first Señor Ferrari didn't want to give in: Elsa was just for him, and no one else could play her part (no one else in the world, he said, and I think at the end he liked her better than the real one). But you know, sir, how hard it is to say no to a president, and even more so in those days; besides, afterward Señor Ferrari had his rewards. He told us she had gone to the capital for an appendix operation, that she had had an attack. But she, a foreigner, and from a humble family, besides, told us everything herself; she thought being with a president was much more important than being *Ingri Berman*. That was the only time anything like that happened with her, but in order to protect himself in the future, even though he had her pretty well under his thumb with his fortune, Señor Ferrari made her sign another contract with strict penalties if she didn't live up to the terms."

"Play it again, Sam," the other man suddenly pronounced, as though to himself. He had abandoned his books and was looking straight ahead once more, shaking his head in controlled desperation. "Play . . . it . . . again . . . Sam . . . Sammy," he repeated after a few moments, mockingly and with a voice increasingly like Bogart's. The black man folded his arms and kept staring at him. The phony Rick perceived that something had caught our attention, so he exaggerated his attitude of desolation. But he smiled immediately, putting on his eyeglasses. Then, without turning his head toward us, he asked, "You still there, *mister?* Do you know what Valéry said? I'll translate it for you, in case you don't. 'God made man, and then, seeing he wasn't lonely enough, he created woman.' Did you hear me?"

I didn't get the connection, and the piano player shook his head indicating that I shouldn't respond. Immediately he got up, leaving our table in order to sit on the piano bench; from there he signaled me to bring over a chair. When I sat down beside him, he struck another very loud chord (the other man smiled, but it was more like a grimace, slumping a bit in his chair), and he gently began to play the song from the beginning.

"Poor Rick," he resumed, without interrupting the piece and with a touch of insincerity in his voice. "You should've seen him, sir, on opening night, when Señor Ferrari brought the cream of Buenos Aires here; even the men couldn't take their eyes off him. Finally Señor Ferrari had to step in so they'd all go back to their seats and the show could go on. But wherever Rick went, there were always more people, especially women (you don't realize, sir, what they were like). That's why later Señor Ferrari had to write him another contract, just like with Elsa; the society ladies wanted to invite him to their ranches, to Europe, anywhere at all; they drowned him in gifts. But Rick was always easygoing; he would rather read than run around with women. Only once that I know of did he get all excited—with that Englishwoman I told you about. She was a stewardess, and whenever she came to Argentina, Señor Ferrari put her up at his ranch so that she could get together with Rick. One day Rick proposed to her; from that time on, she never showed up around here again. That's when Rick started drinking. Señor Ferrari kept him in check, but he didn't forbid him to drink, because that (and especially thinking about that woman) made him seem even more like the movie character. I used to talk to him a lot in those days. Then he started drinking less and took up reading again. Because Rick—I forgot to tell you—was a high school teacher in the Floresta district of Buenos Aires when he met Señor Ferrari; he taught literature and things like that. Señor Ferrari already had the idea in his head to set up this place, so he got Rick's personal information on some pretense or other but didn't tell him anything. He brought him here when this place was almost finished, and Rick couldn't refuse him; Señor Ferrari's offer convinced him right away. He got here just before I did. Around that time, they tell me, Elsa was already here; then came Strasser (they had fixed him and Victor up with surgery, and they were still walking around with bandages on); Renault was already here, and Victor, like I was saying, and so was the girl who played the Spanish singer and the one who played Rick's girlfriend; the waiters were here, the bartender, the little old man who played the maître d' and who had been one in real life. But Ugarte and I arrived practically together; someone spotted him in a flea-joint cabaret where he was singing tangos, and they gave the information to Señor Ferrari (I'm telling you, Señor Ferrari had been looking for people to play the parts for two years; he had talent scouts everywhere, even overseas. Rick and I were the only ones he discovered himself). The orchestra that played with me later on (that cymbal, sir, is all that's left of that orchestra) had already rehearsed with the Brazilian in a room upstairs, where they set up Rick's office later on. When I saw everyone, I knew it couldn't fail—who wouldn't want to be with people that were the spitting image of those in the movie and in a place like the one on screen, besides? I told Señor Ferrari about my hunch, and he laughed; he told me that, in truth, this Casablanca had been created for an audience of one. I didn't exactly understand what he meant until later, when I found out what was going on in a suite of rooms he had built half a block from here, near where we lived, very luxurious rooms that were a copy of the Paris apartment where Rick and Elsa were lovers.

"But I'm getting ahead of myself, sir; sometimes it's hard for me to play the piano and talk at the same time. Like I was telling you today, time—it bites into you and it won't let go. But even though it's very hard for me to talk about it, it's lovely to tell you all this to music; I can see you appreciate it. Well, then, where were we? Oh yes, the first few days we were here. At that time, Señor Ferrari made us watch the movie two or three times a day; he had built a small movie theater that's still there (right next to this house—I don't know if you noticed it when you arrived), which was going to be useful later on. I didn't watch it so often because I had to practice the piano a lot, and also—without being immodest, sir—because it was easy for me to play Sam. An actor Señor Ferrari brought in to teach us acting (a gringo who spoke good Spanish) said I was born to play Sam, so I didn't have to work much with him, either; I just learned to say my lines well in English, because Señor Ferrari wanted us to speak that language. In spite of everything, I don't know if the people who came here could really hear our parts. Señor Ferrari didn't let them crowd all together on the side where the main characters were; he wanted it to be just like in the film: if somebody happened to be close by when Rick was in a scene with Elsa, or with me, or when I was talking to Elsa, or when Rick was meeting with Strasser and Renault, lucky for him; but if he was far away, he had no choice but to return later on and try to get a better seat—half of the available tables were for guests, and the extras, in costume, took the other half. Many of them were workers on Señor Ferrari's lands. The day we opened, for instance, everyone gathered together where the main action was going on. Like I think I told you, we had to interrupt everything and start again. 'This is just like the movie. This is the movie in real life,' Señor Ferrari would say as he pushed the people back into their seats. Finally we were able to continue, but we didn't pay as much attention to details as we should have. That night Señor Ferrari couldn't sleep. Early the next day, he locked himself in a room with the man who had done the decorations and the wardrobe woman, and that afternoon he announced that everything was going to be repainted and redecorated. Every object, including the costumes, was going to be the same color as in the movie; that is, everything was going to be in black and white, with shades of gray, of course, and they were going to make us up in the same shades (as you can imagine, I was spared this trouble; all they did was make me look a little bit older. And I don't know what they did with the ones who had blue or green eyes, but you couldn't notice the color). Luckily, it all came off pretty well; the people who started coming when we re-opened were impressed with that monotone, and you didn't have to struggle much with them. In fact, in those days, some of them even said it felt like they were dreaming. Then, a little while later, since in spite of everything there were always some complaints, Señor Ferrari introduced another new idea: three or four times every evening we would repeat the most important scenes, and each time a different group would sit right up close to where the main actors were. I remember that the men's favorite scene was the one where they arrest Ugarte; the women's was the meeting between Rick and Elsa; and everyone liked the one where Rick gets drunk and makes Sam play the song again, and then Elsa comes back to explain why she left him in Paris. Here, in this part, Señor Ferrari taught Rick to add the word "again" to the dialogue, because when we repeated it, it sounded more natural for him to say, "Play it again, Sam." And for the first meeting between Elsa and Rick, Señor Ferrari went even farther: he said we weren't going to follow the script, that the look between them would last much longer than in the movie and that this song I'm playing right now was going to be the background music, not the orchestra; then he cut out the part where Rick orders Sam to stop playing. So I would keep going, but playing like this, a little more slowly (can you tell the difference?) in order to give the different groups time to get comfortable, and I would repeat the same few bars, singing, because we discovered that the audience didn't want plain music without words when Rick and Elsa looked at each other.

You must remember this,
A kiss is just a kiss,
A sigh is just a sigh . . .

I sang like this, without rushing, just exactly as I played, and you could hear the women sighing like a double bass. What a song, sir! No one wanted it to end, and me less than anyone else. Because I told you about Rick, sir, but I don't know how to describe what happened to everyone when Elsa entered, what happened to me when she greeted me and after asking me where Rick was, looked at me and told me to play this song. The person speaking to me then wasn't the same girl I ran into during the day; it was *Ingri Berman* herself, the spitting image. I don't know how she managed to transform herself like that. She told me to play, and my fingers found the keys, God knows how, because I couldn't take my eyes off her. Then, as you know, she wanted me to sing, and I heard my voice coming from far away, like it belonged to somebody else. What a woman, sir! An angel, even the women in the audience said so. Or a queen, or . . ."

"Damned boy! *Maldito muchacho!* I told you not to let go of my arm. What if I broke a damned bone? Huh? What if I broke something?"

The harsh, hoarse female voice burst into the room along with the squeaking of the door. The black man stopped speaking and playing, leaned backwards and directed a very sober glance toward the entrance. A gust of air extinguished the candle flames, and just then, at the front of the room there appeared the silhouette of a woman dressed in white, wearing a hat; as she walked, she leaned on the boy I had seen earlier. Her face was veiled in a piece of gray tulle that hung from the hat to her waist; the boy carried a folded red umbrella. They stopped halfway across the room. The woman tilted her head a bit to the side as if to get a better view through the tulle, and then that voice could be heard again:

"Oh, come on, Sam, damn it! Did you get me out of bed for nothing? On a night like this? For nothing, Sam!" she said very hoarsely and ill-humoredly in an accent I couldn't quite place.

The piano player hesitated, then raising his hands as if to excuse himself, finally replied, "Elsa, this gentleman is a journalist who's made a special trip from Buenos Aires to learn about our Casablanca."

I stiffened when I heard what he had called her. She began to approach me, still leaning on the boy, who never took his eyes off her. I recognized her outfit immediately: it was a combination of several that Bergman wore in the film: the white dress with buttoned sleeves that she wore when she came back to talk to Rick the same night she met with him when the café was already closed; the piece of tulle covering her head in that same scene; the striped shirt (here peeking out from the décolletage of the dress); the white saucer hat, the gloves and sandals she wore when she went with

Victor to see Strasser; the brooch and the envelope purse she carried in her first scene. She stood next to a table a few feet from us; the boy, without leaving her side, brought over a chair and helped her sit down. She tossed her purse on the table, and with majestic annoyance removed her gloves; then, sitting very erect, slowly turned her head in all directions as if to inspect the place. The boy once again stood by the cymbal from the percussion set.

"Ilsa Lund, sir," Sam suddenly announced, and as I tried to direct my eyes toward him, he returned to the piano and very quietly began playing another song from the movie. The woman appeared not to notice; her veiled face kept scanning the room as though she had nothing to do with us. But just then she turned to the piano player.

"*Hello, Sam,*" she greeted him in a very sweet voice that, to my great surprise, was no longer hoarse.

"*Hello, Miss Ilsa. I never expected to see you again,*" he replied in perfect English without turning around, like someone responding to a familiar stimulus.

The woman nodded her head very slightly, as though insinuating a smile behind the veil, glanced toward the bar, and then, skipping a few lines of the script, inquired in the same tone, "*Where is Rick?*"

The piano player replied, again in English, using the words from the film, that he hadn't seen him all night.

The woman's head moved very slightly once more.

"*You used to be a much better liar, Sam,*" she admonished, skipping a few paragraphs and caressing him with her voice.

The black man, as his role indicated, continued playing and acting evasive. But then, as he was about to respond, she cut him short.

"*Play it once, Sam, for old times' sake.*"

"*I don't know what you mean, Miss Ilsa,*" he replied, exactly as the actor did in the movie.

"*Play it, Sam. Play 'As Time Goes By,'*" she insisted, and I couldn't take my eyes off her table. I thought I was listening to the actress.

The black man, just like the character who plays the piano, replied that he didn't remember that song ("*I can't remember it, Miss Ilsa. I'm a little rusty on it,*" he said with the same perfect pronunciation).

"*I'll hum it for you,*" she persisted, immediately beginning to hum the song in a soft voice. Then he began to play her request.

For a few seconds, the woman listened, her face resting in her hand; then she asked, *"Sing it, Sam."*

And the black man began to sing:

You must remember this
A kiss is just a kiss,
A sigh is just a sigh.
The fundamental things apply
As time goes by . . .

I looked at the phony Rick, since next came the scene where he was supposed to appear and interrupt Sam (I had forgotten what the piano player had told me about the suppression of that incident), but he was dozing again, just as I had found him when I came in.

"Hello, Rick," the woman greeted him, nonetheless.

I turned around, looked at her, and instantly my eyes clouded over. She had lifted the veil, and the face observing me (ironically, but with a *kindly* sort of irony) was Ingrid Bergman's face. An older version, like Rick's, but exactly the same as the actress's face. Almost in tears, I registered those intensely blue eyes, that wavy, chestnut hair, that mouth, still full enough not to need the excess lipstick it wore; that expression, in short, which was so typical of that woman whose most insignificant portrait has always seduced me. I looked at her (I contemplated her, a mystic would say), fascinated, for I don't know how long; I only know that when the veil covered her once more, my eyes were seeing, not the face of an old woman, but rather the marvelous countenance that appears in the film.

"Boy!" she cried out again in a voice that was once more hoarse and authoritarian.

The child ran over to give her his arm. The piano player, distracted, continued playing and singing. With the confused feeling of seeing an image belonging to some old, already forgotten dream now become real, I observed the woman and the boy heading for the door. I followed them with my eyes till they disappeared behind the stack of chairs.

"I'm going to the movies, Sam. Good night, Mr. . . . *journalist.* You got here a few years too late," I heard her say by way of farewell, but I can't be sure if she said it before or after she vanished from sight.

The black man stopped playing and stared at the piano in silence. After nodding his head a few times, he turned toward the entrance, and, with his hands on his knees, as though he were dreaming, he began to speak.

"Did you see, sir, what a woman she is? Can you imagine what she was like at thirty? At forty, even at fifty? ... Did you see her legs, her calves? ... With a bit of luck, poor Elsa could go around in a bathing suit even today. I saw her, sir," he added, sighing, and seeking me out with his gaze, "at all those ages I mentioned, but I don't know when she was most beautiful. And not only beautiful, also quite intelligent. I don't think she believed the story about you being a journalist (excuse me for lying). But she liked you; usually she won't take the trouble to say one word for an audience of less than ten. At most she shows up to let people have a look at her, but no one can get a word out of her. I always tell her even *one* person is important, that it all adds up, but she doesn't pay me any mind. I don't know what happened to her with you; she even greeted you as if you were Rick, did you notice? I know her well, sir, you must be someone special, someone generous, I mean. Women recognize that right away."

He stopped, and as if trying to disguise all those self-interested remarks a bit, looked once more toward the spot where the woman had disappeared. I took advantage of the opportunity to ask what she had meant by the movies.

"Ah, the movies," he said, laughing. "The movie theater I told you about just now. The one Señor Ferrari built so that those people who weren't familiar with the film could see it before coming into this place. That way they could understand what was going on in here and finish it off with what was going on outside, I mean in the streets of Casablanca, in Paris, at Renault's place—the 'outside shots,' our boss called them. We still have a pretty good copy of the film, and Elsa likes to watch it every once in a while. Because (just between us, sir), she thinks she's the actress. More than once I've caught her grumbling and remarking while she was watching the movie and thought she was alone, that she had made a mistake in this or that scene, that she was careless and other worse stuff. And it's not that she's gone crazy or anything; a doctor who came here recently to see the show and who stayed afterward talking to me explained that she thinks this way because she's alive and the real actress isn't; she was becoming something like the continuation of the woman on the screen. That's what the man said. I don't know, sir, but maybe he's right, because I can remember quite well how she reacted the day she found out *Ingri* had died; she locked herself in her room for three or four days, and when she came out, she wasn't the same anymore; she had delusions of grandeur, she was rude to all of us—among other things, she wouldn't let me call her 'Elsa' like I always used to; I had to call her 'Ilsa,' like in the film. I didn't put up an argument because I thought she'd get over it in a little while, but, man, was I ever wrong! Some people got mad at her, and more than one tourist made fun of her when she wouldn't let them take photos of her. Rick and I were among the few people who realized that what she was doing made this place seem more important, made those of us who were here seem more important. Look, there are days when even we believe that the famous actress didn't die, that she's here, growing old along with some of her friends from *Casablanca*. Anyway, that story doesn't hurt anyone, so why stir things up, right?"

He stopped speaking and watched me for a few seconds; then he pulled a handkerchief from his pants pocket and wiped his eyes with it. I observed the lights, which had been flickering a bit more ever since the woman left. The piano player stuck the handkerchief back in his pocket and explained: "We don't have light, but a diesel generator runs the projector. Ugarte operates it; he's been in charge of the movie house ever since he had to retire on account of his weight. These days he runs the movie practically just for Elsa, but before, when there was no video, lots of people used to come to see the movie, because they weren't even showing it in Buenos Aires. Ugarte used to put signs up on the road, and like I'm telling you, lots of tourists would come out to see it. Afterwards, if they wanted, we were on hand to complete their visit with some live performances. The two of them, Elsa and Ugarte, get along real well; they became friends during . . . Oh, sir, what am I thinking, I was about to say during the filming. No, please, I mean during the performances and afterwards, when we had parties and Ugarte knocked himself out dedicating tangos to her. But, well, that's another story, and now we're talking about movie theaters and movies, so I should tell you more about *our* movie."

He stopped talking and smiled briefly at his remark. Then he glanced at the phony Rick, who was sleeping with his mouth open, and continued: "We were talking about Elsa, I think. Yes, what a woman. She's Australian (Señor Ferrari used to call her 'my little kangaroo' when a few drinks made him feel sentimental), and she worked with a North American circus troupe that was traveling through Brazil. A talent scout told Señor Ferrari about her, and when a picture of the girl arrived, Señor Ferrari himself went there to bring her back. Unfortunately, there was a contract involved, so our boss had to shell out a nice sum of money so they'd let her out of it. Here, on his ranch, Señor Ferrari supplied her with a Spanish instructor, an acting instructor, and an instructor in good manners, because whenever she spoke, every other word was a swear word. According to what they told me when I came here, she learned everything they taught her very quickly; I can say that, except for that mouth of hers when she got angry (there was practically nothing anyone could do about that), in every other way she was exactly like the character of Ilsa Lund. So that she'd get accustomed to it, as soon as she arrived, Señor Ferrari made her dress in the clothes the real Elsa wore in the movie, even the underwear . . . Yes, don't look at me like that, like I say—and I'm not lying—she told me almost everything herself after Señor Ferrari died and this place started to fall apart. And don't think I'm fooling myself; the place did fall apart and, if you want to make a comparison with what it used to be, we're living in ruins now. But at least we're living, sir, and we can even entertain people, sure we can, show them a good time while they have a drink. Like I was telling you, Señor Ferrari wanted an Ilsa Lund just like the one in the movie, and he wanted her inside, outside, and underneath . . . her clothing, I mean—please don't get me wrong."

He ventured a sly little laugh, but soon cut it short. He glanced briefly at the portrait on the table and continued.

"Don't think I'm ungrateful, sir, or that I want to make fun of the deceased, airing his dirty laundry in public. But this matter I'm telling you about is also a piece of our Casablanca, the most hidden piece—and again let me repeat, I'm not joking. Because Señor Ferrari loved *Ingri Berman* so much, he even tried to imagine what color underwear she was wearing in this or that scene of *Casablanca*. And so our Elsa had to wear whatever he told her to. According to what she told me, Señor Ferrari used to go crazy whenever she put on a light green bra and panties, green like water, because he said it was the shade that best suited her ivory complexion, the same as the actress's. Even Señor Ferrari told her that no one could convince him that in her first scene in the movie, *Ingri* wasn't wearing that color garment underneath her white outfit; he had an obsession about that. And the guy didn't have to wonder about it either; it wasn't just wishful thinking: because in our Casablanca, anyway, Elsa wore whatever he wanted. I thought it was funny, and when I became friendlier with her, I told her, as a joke, that neither the actor who played Victor Lazslo in the movie nor the famous *Umprey Bogar* could ever have found out what Señor Ferrari knew. But, well, one time (I think I may have mentioned this to you already, right?) he told me that this entire Casablanca had been constructed just for him, and it took me some time to understand what he'd meant. (Truth is, I thought he was referring to his resemblance to Ferrari in the movie, that when he saw how much he looked like the other one, he had the idea of building his own Casablanca, because he was always making jokes about the resemblance; but that wasn't it at all). A while ago I told you about some buildings right around here that were copies of Rick and Elsa's apartment in Paris to the last detail. There, after every show (everything ended when Victor sang the *Marseillaise* along with everyone else and Strasser had the place closed down), the only ones allowed inside were the two main characters. They drank champagne, like in the film, they hugged and kissed, and then Elsa would start to undress, and when she was down to just her shoes and those two garments we were talking about earlier, she would go into the bedroom, where Señor Ferrari waited for her, sitting in an armchair; then Rick, very slowly, would go back to his room, which was right next to mine. Rick or Victor—because Señor Ferrari also built some hotel rooms like those the couple supposedly used in the city of Casablanca, and sometimes he liked to replace Victor instead of Rick—so that Rick wouldn't be the only one hurt, as we boys used to joke. Because all of us, sir, we all found out what was going on in those places, and nobody found it strange. Elsa belonged to Señor Ferrari, and it didn't matter if he slept with her on his ranch or in those rooms. The strange thing . . . the strangest thing (and we learned this later, from Elsa herself) was that he could only 'perform,' in those situations that were a continuation of the film. He even called her 'Ilsa' the whole time he was there with her, in those rooms, sometimes all night long and the next day or next *days* if there was no show. He loved watching her in a housecoat playing the role of Ilsa, watching her reading magazines, cooking, bathing (watching her do her toenails was his weakness) and all those things women do around the house. Later, on performance nights, when it was time to go to the café, he would hand her over to Victor again. This is what our boss had meant, sir. What do you think? Now, only God knows where he got this idea from. True, there were rumors in those days that he had tried his luck with *Ingri Berman* herself (he had offered her his entire fortune, through a messenger) but that she never answered him. And that's why the man felt resentful and invented all this, see? In some ways he was kind of an odd person, and neither I nor anybody else dared ask him anything about that. But excuse me for a second."

He left the bench and headed quickly toward the phony Rick, whose body was about to fall to one side. He moved the books aside, and gently, trying not to awaken him, positioned him with his hands on the table. When he thought he was comfortable, he returned to the bench and continued his story.

"Like I was telling you, Señor Ferrari could only get it up when he met with Elsa here, in Casablanca; in his real house, the one at the ranch, or even when they traveled somewhere, he didn't feel like touching her. She liked it like that, and yet she didn't. It was okay with her because that way Señor Ferrari showed her she *was Ingri Berman*; but on the other hand, it made her furious that Pamela Robinson (that was her real name) couldn't get a rise out of him. Women's stuff, sir, because, what more could she want? He only bothered her once in a while and just 'in' a film, you might say . . . The thing is, around that time she already had more on her mind than the salary, gifts, and trips Señor Ferrari gave her. What I'm telling you about must have been around the second or third year after we started here. But remember the old saying: Man calculates or proposes . . . and God disposes. It was all smooth sailing when one day hoof-and-mouth disease broke out among Señor Ferrari's livestock; what happened to the animals was a disaster. And as though that wasn't enough, the rains came and flooded everything; here, where we are right now, we had about a foot-and-a-half of water. We had to cancel the shows for a couple of months, and when Casablanca reopened (for winter vacation that year), we all felt like we had been hit by something; it just wasn't the same. Señor Ferrari didn't say a word, he tried to put a good face on it, as they say, to act like nothing had happened. But Elsa was the first one to notice that something *had* happened; the gifts were fewer and cheaper, the trips no longer took them very far away. One weekend Señor Ferrari informed us that the Saturday and Sunday shows that week would be canceled because he had to go to the Capital to meet with the president, General Perón.

"He came back on Tuesday, and after gathering us all together, he broke the news: from now on we were to play for real money at the roulette wheel and the poker tables, not for worthless tokens like we'd done till then. We were all surprised; the only licensed casino in the province of Buenos Aires was the one in Mar del Plata, and I think there was also another one in Necochea. But he said we weren't going to have any problems, that's what friends were for (I remember how Elsa smiled, sir, just like it was yesterday, when she heard the word *friends*). Then a lot of money started coming in, and we thought everything would go back to being like before. But, truth is, that windfall wasn't even noticeable here. Señor Ferrari planned to build more places and hire script writers to write those scenes that began after the ones in the movie ended, like for example the one where Elsa gets undressed. He wanted to build a little headquarters for the Gestapo, to see what happened after they arrested Ugarte; he wanted to create Renault's police station and also Ferrari's Arabian café from the movie; he even wanted to construct the airport for the final scene, when Ilsa and Victor escape (on opening night he had a crop-duster fly overhead, but then he had the scene painted on a giant canvas that lit up as the audience left); anyway, as he sometimes remarked, from one single film he wanted to make two or three. But after the hoof-and-mouth business and the water, even though he started to recover, like I said, with the roulette wheel and poker, he never mentioned those plans again. That's when we realized his situation was worse than it seemed. Luckily, he was never late in paying us, but somehow you got the feeling maybe Señor Ferrari's dream wouldn't last much longer. In spite of it all, everything continued more or less the same for a few more seasons. But in fifty-five, the military threw Perón out of office, and what came after was worse than the hoof-and-mouth and the rain combined: the gambling business collapsed.

"As usual, Señor Ferrari didn't say anything. But one Monday, late in the afternoon, after a weekend with very few customers, he locked himself up in here with orders for no one to disturb him. Right away there was a rumor that something was the matter with the boss, and then we started gathering outside the door. We were discussing what to do when we heard the shot. It was a while before anyone dared go inside. Elsa, who was at the ranch where Señor Ferrari had sent her on some phony excuse, arrived when the highway patrol was already here examining the body. She didn't want to go in; she went to the rooms that were supposed to be the French apartment and locked herself up inside until they took the body away. She didn't go to the wake or the funeral, either. They buried Señor Ferrari in the Mar del Plata cemetery, the old one, and just about a month ago Elsa went there to bring him flowers."

He grew silent and turned toward the piano. He struck the edge of the keys with one finger, adjusted himself on the bench and began playing the song clumsily; soon the melody broke up into a series of disconnected sounds. He kept on playing this way for a few seconds, and the parody finally concluded with a sweeping motion along the keys with the back of his hand. After that, he turned toward me and with a weary smile, explained:

"What you just heard on the piano, sir, is what happened to us, what happened to this Casablanca when Señor Ferrari died. Something worse than the hoof-and-mouth, or the rains. The sky fell down on us, as they say. We didn't know which way to turn. To top it all off, soon after that, a law clerk showed up to inform us that, before he killed himself, Señor Ferrari had sold all his land, because he had to pay for the damage the hoof-and-mouth had done to his animals and for the crops that were ruined by the floods (we found out he had invested all his savings in Casablanca). The only thing left unsold was this part where we are now, and in his will, he put down that it was for us, but only on condition we carry on like before, or if that wasn't possible, that at the very least we shouldn't change the buildings at all. He wanted Casablanca to continue until, as the law clerk read, 'it was worn away by wind and rain.' To everyone's surprise (most of all mine), he named me the one responsible for carrying out his wishes and named the law clerk executor if I did things right. This news was a bit of a relief, although just a bit, because believe me, like the saying goes, it's hard for a poor man to have fun. Two or three days after talking to the law clerk, some soldiers showed up here to investigate the roulette business and our relations with the Perón government. But we were just employees, so they were satisfied with watching a free show and having a few drinks on the house, and then they closed the building for an indefinite length of time.

"That really did us in: we had been planning to form a cooperative and keep the business going; someone would come along to replace Señor Ferrari—I mean his character, of course. In order to meet expenses and survive, we had to make do with what we'd saved. Two or three times a week, Elsa and Rick would go to La Plata to see if they could get the closure order reversed, but all they accomplished was to make the officials joke about how much they resembled the actors. Eventually Elsa went by herself. Until one day she showed up in a car belonging to some Navy officer, all smiles. She got out of the car, and the first thing she did was yell 'Shit!'; then she tore up the closure order page by page. Inside the car, the officer's chauffeur, a corporal, was laughing. So, then we took off again, still without anyone to play Ferrari (his scenes weren't all that popular, so it didn't matter to us that much), and our savings got used up with the advertising we had to do to make up for all the time we'd been closed. At first the thing looked like it was going to take off, but after a few months, we were still in the red; it was impossible to maintain the salaries we had agreed on as a cooperative, much less those we had been earning before. Besides, sir, there was something else going on here that was even more poisonous than the subject of money: now, in the 'French' apartment, Elsa had to take her clothes off for the officer who had helped her with reversing the closure order. He had taken Señor Ferrari's place, and he convinced her to throw parties here with other soldiers and other women after the performances. It was as though a plague had struck our Casablanca. After a while, Victor (he was Mexican, but not one of those macho types, not at all), Renault, Strasser, and even Rick himself helped make sure the foundations of our co-op went slowly but surely to hell.

One night, Elsa announced that her Navy officer boyfriend had been named ambassador of some country or other around here, in South America, and that she was going with him. Our co-op agreement was verbal; no one had signed anything (Señor Ferrari's death had left all of us free—and out on the street), but regardless, Rick, Ugarte and I talked to her. Elsa cried, called herself a traitor, insulted herself in every language possible, offered us the jewelry Señor Ferrari had given her, but she didn't give an inch. After two or three days, she took off with all her luggage . . . and all her jewelry. The only thing left in the 'French' apartment were the costumes she had worn in the shows. That's when the rats started abandoning ship, sir. Suddenly everyone found a new job, especially the musicians and the ones who had bit parts; as far as the extras were concerned (we had to give raises to those who were Señor Ferrari's employees so they'd stay on after their boss's suicide, but they all wanted to leave, anyway), like I was saying, as far as the extras were concerned, hardly a single one of them remained. Without really understanding what had happened, one perfectly ordinary afternoon we realized that there were only six or seven of us left in Casablanca: Rick, Ugarte, Strasser, Renault, Yvonne (Rick's girlfriend in the story and Strasser's in real life), Victor (one of the waiters, a boy who hadn't been here too long, had been his reason for staying), me, and the croupier, I think. I remember quite well how we all gathered at the bar and started uncorking bottles. By the time we woke up, it was already seven o'clock the next morning, and we were all sprawled out on the floor. But it was just a way of letting off steam; soon we had to start thinking about what we were going to do with this white elephant, as Rick always called it . . . What's wrong, Fortu? Where's Elsa?"

Without our realizing it (the dampness produced by the rain kept the hinges from creaking), the boy had entered the room and was walking very slowly toward us, the folded umbrella in his hand.

"Ugarte used up all his diesel for the scene where Ilsa and Victor are with Ferrari in the Blue Parrot. Miss Elsa is outside, watching the door," the boy explained from halfway down the corridor.

"Go with her, quick, back to the house," the piano player said brusquely. The boy ran toward the entrance.

"These young snots today . . . I've told him not to leave her side when he walks with her," he grumbled without taking his eyes off the entryway. "And let's hope the diesel story isn't just something Ugarte made up. Sometimes he likes to go to bed early, and since he doesn't have the guts to say no to Elsa, he invents things," he added, leaning back on his piano bench. But immediately he leaned forward again in order to observe the entrance. The candle flames flickered, and, following the sound of footsteps, the woman and the boy reappeared at the end of the corridor, with her clutching his arm. This time, her face was uncovered, and she looked at the room as if she had never seen it before. When they stopped for her to get a closer view of some detail, her eyes reflected a sort of pained surprise. They walked up to us silently, and she regarded the piano player inquisitively, as though he looked familiar. From there they went over to the table where the phony Rick was sitting; the woman leaned over a bit in order to see him better; then she smiled and brushed his head with her hand. They continued on toward the bar, she gazing at everything with that surprised expression, and from there they retraced their steps. The black man observed her somberly. They started down the corridor toward the entrance, and halfway there, she picked up one of the kerosene lanterns from a table.

"Lately she's been doing the same thing whenever she sees the movie," Sam confided in a whisper, leaning slightly toward me. "She doesn't recognize this place, or else she thinks she's dreaming, I don't know. Whenever I ask her about it later, she tells me she doesn't have any idea what I'm talking about."

They continued down the hallway, with the lantern in her hand. They stopped before making their way around the stack of chairs; she raised the lantern a bit, turned her head toward us and looked at me—I felt as though a portrait of the actress had come to life, and I meekly surrendered to those eyes whose penetrating blue were intensified by the lamplight and distance. When I recovered from the weakness this exchange had caused me, she and the boy had vanished.

"The years, sir, the years; I never get tired of repeating it. Like that tango goes, 'they make you want to crawl into a corner and shoot yourself,'" the piano player added, unaware of what was happening inside me. Somehow I could still see the woman's eyes before me. However, I reacted with a smile, and he went off to get the glasses we had left on the table. He poured what remained in the bottle of gin, a little in each glass, returned to his bench, and continued.

"As I was explaining to you, the problem was what to do with this place. We spoke to some people (the ones who had bought the land, for example) in order to see if it could be set afloat again with a little capital, but every one of them said Señor Ferrari's project had been madness, delirium. We realized we were alone, and to top it all off, there was no solution. Even worse, some tourists who had seen the posters came by and the only thing we could offer them were a few drinks and our apologies. Later on, even the apologies disappeared and there were just the drinks; Señor Ferrari's Casablanca had become just another one of the many bars along the route. Rick and the other boys who had major parts let their beards grow or disfigured themselves some other way, so it wouldn't look like they were leftovers from something that had once been important. Me, I stayed the same as before, playing the piano and introducing myself as Sam, because it was only right that the black piano player from the film should be the symbol of a bar called Casablanca.

We went on like that for I don't know how long, barely making enough to eat and pay our expenses. Rick tended bar; Ugarte waited tables. Strasser couldn't take it anymore and went off with Yvonne to try their luck in Peru, she as an actress on the radio and he as a German professor (he was the son of Czech parents and he spoke that language well). Victor stayed behind on account of the boy who used to play the waiter during the good times and who now made the sandwiches and things like that; but one day Victor found him lying in the grass with a worker and he took off without saying goodbye; we never saw him again. Renault kept books and was in charge of paying bills and taxes, and Raúl, the croupier, had the job of advertising our place along the route. I think those of us who were still here at that time already knew (I don't know how we knew, but we did) that we would never leave. Besides, after Perón fell, we heard things were getting very rough everywhere, that there was no work for anyone. And here, at least, we could manage; there was no shortage of food. It was the lesser evil, sure, but it was also Casablanca, and I don't know which of those two things was more important.

"And so, between this and that, several years went by, and slowly, very slowly, the audience started changing. We started getting mostly truckers, don't ask me why. They didn't know anything about the movie, so gradually I stopped playing, and I didn't play Sam, either; I saved that for times when a better class of people visited, people who had been referred or who recognized the name and the outside of the place enough to understand what it was all about. But the truth is that the truckers were the important thing in those days. At their request (some of them were on their way to Patagonia and needed a place to rest), we began to rent them the rooms that had belonged to the help who worked at Casablanca, to us. Rick and I moved to the 'French' apartment, which has two large rooms; Renault and the other two boys, the waiter and the croupier, took over the 'hotel' in the city of Casablanca; Ugarte decided to set up a room for himself in the movie theater; because of his weight, which he couldn't control anymore, he concentrated on showing the movie. After a little while, the truckers started bringing women they picked up on the road—'roadies,' as we call them. We looked the other way, because our expenses and taxes were higher all the time. But the word spread, and the people who had bought Señor Ferrari's land told the law clerk and threatened to report us. We had to have it out with the truckers, but we had no other choice. That, sir, was another critical moment for us and for this place. The truckers organized a boycott right away, and the whole thing got very ugly. We ran around like crazy, hanging posters with the word *Casablanca* everywhere, and Ugarte rushed to get the movie theater up and running. Rick and I rehearsed a few scenes, and that kept us afloat for a while; we even got an offer to act in a cabaret in Mar del Plata. But we didn't accept, and if you ask me why (truth is, we didn't think about it too much before turning it down), I'd have to tell you that this place is like a femme fatale; for us, it's what *Ingri Berman* was for Señor Ferrari. But, well, going back to what we were talking about, I can't say exactly how long the two of us kept Casablanca and our partners going all by ourselves. It took a lot of work to refurbish Ugarte's movie theater, but at last it opened, and that helped all of us. He wanted to show only *Casablanca,* but later he had to add cowboy movies, because that's what the farm workers around here liked. The poor guy grew bitter and even fatter. But we ended up lending him a hand; there were people who knew the movie only by name, and when they saw Rick and me acting, they wanted to know where we had gotten those scenes from, and then they went over to Ugarte's place. That's why it wasn't long before he could start showing only *Casablanca* again.

"Yes, a lot of things happened, but I won't bore you with the details of our suffering, until the time we saw Elsa again. Fourteen years, not a day less. One day when I was touching up the paint on a poster of a Marrakesh policeman that we keep at the front door, I heard a woman saying, "Sam, *sanababich!*" I turned, but no one was there. Then I heard the voice again, and behind it a woman came out from between some trees, shouting and laughing. It was her, Elsa. She acted as though nothing had happened. At first I wanted to act tough, and I didn't even give her a smile. But it didn't matter—even if she had killed my mother, believe me, I would have (I think anyone would have) ended up forgiving her anyway; the vibes she sent out were too much for any man. She had changed her hairstyle and had gained a few pounds that looked very good on her. The other boys (Rick, Ugarte, Renault . . .) held out even less than I did, and just a little while after she arrived, they started bombarding her with questions. She told us her affair with the Navy guy had lasted just three months; when he raised his hand to her one time, she dumped him. She went to Mexico, and from there to North America; she wanted to work in the movies. She managed to land something here and there, but everyone advised her to play *Ingri's* double, and, according to what she told us, she finally took that advice. (She wanted to make us believe it was no big deal for her to take that job, that she was happy to do it, but I know, sir, it couldn't have been easy for her.) She worked—according to her—in a movie with *Ingri,* as her double, and she did it so well that once, when the actress was tired, she sent her to film a scene in her place; and it seems the director didn't even notice, so in one part of that movie (don't ask me which one—I'm terrible with names), Elsa appears instead of *Ingri.* After that film, a producer promised to hire her, not as a double, but as an actress, but—according to what she told us—the producer had an accident, and the project was abandoned."

"All set, Godfather. Can I stay?" the boy asked suddenly, interrupting us. He had returned silently and was standing by the entrance.

"What about Miss Elsa? Did you take her home?" the piano player asked him, somewhat severely.

"Yes, Godfather. Renault helped her inside, and he's with her now."

Sam nodded approval, motioning him over.

"Renault is her neighbor at the 'hotel,' and even though he's not well, he can still lend her a hand if she needs it," the black man explained as the boy sat down beside the phony Rick. "But we were talking about when Elsa first came back after she went away. That time, the first time, I mean, she stayed only a few days and disappeared again. She showed up again around ten years later, maybe nineteen-eighty, if I recall correctly. She told us about all this fancy stuff—trips, love affairs, successes with this and that—and talked about staying this time and reviving Casablanca, which in those days was pretty run down; we could barely scrape enough together to pay the electric bill or fix something when it got broken or worn out. From the way she talked and how she looked, we understood that things hadn't gone too well for her, either. We let her explain her plans to us a little, but only for the pleasure of listening to her; none of us really was about to argue or create obstacles for her. Suddenly, sir, we felt—well, protected—with her nearby.

"Right away we started rehearsing her scenes with Rick, like in the old days, and that part was the special attraction we began to offer the public. And you wouldn't believe how our audiences grew, the numbers. Because we didn't have money for publicity, but people showed up anyway, as if they had smelled something important waiting for them here. Five years, sir, our success lasted five years—a modest success, sure, very modest if you compare it with what we had before, when Señor Ferrari was alive, but not so modest if you stack it up against the time when we were really starving. Five years later, like I was just saying, a magazine photographer who had seen our show convinced Elsa to go to Buenos Aires to do some nude shots posing as *Ingri* (it was the time the 'lid' came off, remember? After the soldiers from the dictatorship left and all the women wanted to get undressed, even the old ones). She told us she'd be back in a few days. We suspected something was fishy because she took almost all her clothing. And, in fact, we weren't mistaken; the 'few days' became more than a year. This time she showed up hanging her head; she hardly spoke (not a word about the magazine photos). We didn't ask any questions (when she came in smiling, she won us over, and now she won us over in a different way: we were all like her father), but we just went on as if nothing had happened. But Señor Ferrari had been right when he said that once a hit is interrupted, you can't get it back again; we proved him right with our own hides. This time, things were just as incredible, but incredible in the opposite way: hardly anyone showed up, and even though we offered the same show with the same people, it didn't have the same appeal as before. I don't know what kind of spell had been cast on us. Truth is, sir, we all started to feel like ending this business, going somewhere else, I don't know, Buenos Aires, the capital. But we had a meeting and we all talked and talked, and the only thing we got out of it was that at the bottom of our hearts, no one really wanted to leave. Finally, we all got drunk almost like that time before, and the next day, the disaster that was weighing on us didn't seem so serious or so dangerous—look what drink can do, sir."

As he uttered the last sentence, he left the piano bench for the table we had occupied earlier. He took the bottle of gin and upended it; two or three drops spilled out.

"Well, we can't complain; the two of us emptied a bottle all by ourselves," he said, feigning indifference as he returned to the piano bench. He placed the bottle on the edge of the piano, looking at the phony Rick (who was snoring quietly) and at the boy, who was thumbing through one of the books. Realizing that I was watching him, he began to read (to massacre, really), the French text:

"Cess la mel-lure . . . cour-si-er . . . lay . . . mel-lure . . . car-ro . . . car-ros-sey . . . pour say voy-tour-ray . . ." he pronounced slowly, without raising his voice and glancing toward my chair again and again.

"Read to yourself, Fortunato, you'll wake Rick," Sam ordered, and the boy immediately hid his face behind the book. "It's better to let him sleep, because otherwise he'll be wanting his food, and it's not ready yet. But I was telling you . . . I was telling you . . ."

"That you all got drunk," I offered.

"Oh, yes. Right. We got drunk just like other people take a bath when something bad happens to them—in order to scrub off all that bad luck. Because I don't know what else to call it, sir. To flop with something that had been a hit . . . But, well, now I remember where I was. The booze helped us kind of get rid of our fear, and we understood (Rick said it very well the next day) that doing our job badly would have been a failure, but doing it well and not getting an audience in spite of everything, wasn't our problem, like Rick said . . . 'God knows why it happened.' Anyway, I don't want to bother you with something that's neither here nor there. I'd rather tell you about the last 'act' of our *movie*.

"So we gathered up our strength from who knows where and kept on going. Around then the law clerk died, and his son, who was in the same profession, came to see us. At first he was a little angry at the way this place had supposedly been neglected; but later he promised to help us, saying that with a little money everything could be resolved. Finally—and this is the good part—he told us he was looking for someone he could give a child to—a baby, because the mother had died in childbirth and the father couldn't bring him up. Nobody here said yes or no, but the next day he showed up with the kid, and we were won over. Elsa said we should name him Fortunato, because that name would bring him—and us—good luck. And look, sir, she was right, because no sooner did the boy arrive here than things started to work out better; we stopped swinging in the wind a bit. And who can say? Maybe he's the one responsible for saving you from the storm tonight; I mean, if the law clerk hadn't brought him, who knows what might have happened to this business. So you might say several of us owe poor Fortunato something."

And having said this, he gazed at the boy, who moments before had put his book aside in order to listen to the piano player's story. On hearing his name, the boy hung his head, showing an unexpected interest in the design of the floor. Sam smiled and added, raising his voice slightly, "But you can't cut too much slack with him; if you do, he'll bolt like a colt."

The boy glanced at me for a moment and then continued tracing the pattern of the floor tiles with his foot.

"As for the law clerk, the son," he continued after clearing his throat, "he never came by here with anything resembling the money. We had to get by on our wits and with the blessings this child brought us. Because, I repeat, we weren't lacking for good fortune. And by this time, the only ones working were Rick, Elsa, and myself. Renault, who had been just a decoration for the last few years (he would sit in the middle of the room in his white uniform, just to let the public see him, as 'filler,' like they say), started getting cramps in his legs and couldn't continue. Ugarte was so fat that no one could recognize him anymore, and since videos had put the movies out of business, he helped

Raúl behind the counter. The three of us played the scenes I told you about, and people were satisfied.

"Later on (maybe around five years later), the law clerk brought a deputy from the Province who came to us after the show to discuss a project to declare our Casablanca a place of cultural interest or something like that; we would be named curators, with a salary for each one of us (our performances would be honorary from then on), and the government would pay for electricity, taxes, and upkeep. You can imagine how we reacted to this news. If it hadn't been so hard to replace our liquor supply, I think we would have gotten drunk like the times before, this time from happiness—no matter, we had a glass or two, but without overdoing it. Elsa was the most enthusiastic one of us; she was already planning receptions, cocktail parties, hobnobbing with political big shots. The rest of us had dreams, too, naturally, but it was different: we wanted it to be a way to recognize Señor Ferrari's efforts and for Casablanca to look like it did the first day. That was our fantasy, sir, and the truth is, we were sort of blind, we were like little kids. Around that time, the law clerk started coming here with other people, who according to what he said were the Deputy's team. They took pictures, measurements, and they half-ignored us, like we weren't there or didn't matter very much.

"One morning the Deputy showed up with the law clerk and two other men. They inspected every corner of Casablanca, by themselves (the law clerk made a big deal about not wanting to disturb us). We let them do their thing, even though there was something, something about those people, that I didn't quite like; but since I'm very mistrustful, sir, I told myself that I was getting carried away with my thoughts, and so I didn't make any comment. They left after noon, without saying goodbye to anyone. I didn't like that, either, but I figured maybe it got late and they had to go.

"Three or four days later, the law clerk came to see us. We met right here, where we are now; none of us were missing. He began by pretending to act nice, flirting with Elsa; later, when he saw we weren't laughing, he got more serious. Finally, he laughed one more time and then and there he whipped out the proposal, that dirty trick they had prepared. First he criticized our neglect of the place again (he said the Deputy had been outraged by that); then, as though it really mattered to him, he remarked that maybe without meaning or wanting to we were betraying Señor Ferrari's wishes, and finally, since we didn't say a word, he pulled a typed sheet of paper from his briefcase, explaining that if we wanted the Deputy's project to be carried out, we had to temporarily leave Casablanca; we would have to sign the paper recognizing that our evacuation of the premises (those are my words, sir; he used trickier language) was voluntary, that nobody was forcing us to do it. Before he had finished speaking, even the densest one among us knew that it was a trick. Then, when he stopped talking, we kept quiet. Poor Elsa was trembling with anger, but she didn't say a word. As if we had rehearsed it, we all responded by glaring at him. And, when he tried to hand us the paper, we held our arms behind our backs, all at once, like we were just one person. Then he left the paper there, on top of the bar, telling us we were making a very big mistake, and he headed for the door. Before he got outside, Elsa grabbed the piece of paper and tore it up into little pieces without reading it. The man realized what had happened, but he just kept walking.

"He was back here at Casablanca two days later, with the Deputy and a uniformed commissioner. We met here again, and the Deputy ('You talk to them; they don't want to listen to me,' the law clerk told him, acting insulted) began saying that there had been a misunderstanding between the law clerk and us at the earlier meeting, that this time he himself was going to read what was written so that we'd see it was nothing unusual. He pulled out a sheet of paper just like the other one, put on his glasses, and started reading; the commissioner looked at us like we were criminals. But we didn't pay any attention; as the Deputy read, the only thing going through our minds was the story of our Casablanca, this detail and that; sir, it was like we were watching a movie. And I'll tell you something else. At that moment, one single word buzzed in our bonnets: *eviction;* everything else was like the sound of the wind.

"The man stopped reading, took off his glasses, and looked at us, smiling. Then Elsa took a step forward and said (I was about to say 'spat out'): 'No.' The three of them looked at each other, and the commissioner tried to say something; but the Deputy made a sign for him to shut up. Then he came over to me, patted me on the arm, stepping all over himself like a fool and making it all nice and clear, didn't I agree, that it wasn't healthy for people of a certain age to be working in such a big place, without heat in the winter or fresh air in the summer; if it wouldn't be better to have a smaller room, without all these useless tables and chairs, such a horrible color. Besides—he asked me—playing the good guy, why did we have to live here if we could do the same thing in La Plata, in a nicer place paid for by the government, and with buses that would bring us to performances and then take us back home? Even though it was hard for me, sir, I listened to him respectfully, but the others walked out while he was talking; when he finished, I was here alone with the three of them. Then it occurred to me to pick up Señor Ferrari's picture (I always keep it over the piano), show it to him and tell him that he, our boss, didn't want what they were offering us. Whoa, you should've seen him then! He thought I was kidding. He stuck the paper back in the briefcase and left without another word, quick as a flash. The commissioner was the last one to leave, after promising me we'd see each other again soon. When I heard their car take off, I went to find the others; we had to get ready for what was coming next."

He stopped to whisper to his godson, who had picked up the book again.

"Go put out the water and the other things. And be careful with the salt, okay?" he ordered as the boy looked at him.

"Yes, Godfather," the child said, and, leaving the book with the others on the phony Rick's table, he ran toward the entrance. Sam waited for him to disappear from sight and then continued.

"What was coming next, as I was saying. And I wasn't mistaken, sir, because, something that had never happened before, we started to get all sorts of inspections. But we were prepared; the very day they were here, we decided to put the house in order, as they say. We scraped together every last cent and paid all we owed. Elsa pawned some necklaces Señor Ferrari had given her, and with the money from that we fixed up the bathrooms a little and the road that connects us to the main highway. They had nothing to criticize. (Elsa yelled at some inspectors who came by that she was going to report them and the Deputy to the newspapers). But after that, the police got mixed up in it; they would stop visitors at the front door asking to see their documents or bothering them for any old reason. There was even shooting; one night a car came by and from inside they fired four or five shots at the door (the bullet holes are still there). We were scared, of course, but that brought us even closer together: Elsa, for example, put her very last peso on the table. The only way they'll get us out of here—we used to say to give ourselves courage—is feet first.

"And so, with all these ups and downs (Elsa yelled at the Deputy's representative and scared him away), two or three months went by. We tried to avoid going out to the main road for fear they'd arrest us, but learned what was going on around here from the boy who brought us supplies (for years we've been buying everything from a supplier in Maipú) and also from those people who came to Casablanca in spite of everything. These people, sir, when they found out what was being done to us, sided with us right away and took it upon themselves to spread the news in the capital and everywhere—there were lawyers among them and even judges, I think, and we found out that on more than one occasion one of them had to deal with the police who tried to get smart with them at our front door. So little by little we started to feel less alone, and that helped us to get out of the dumps we sometimes fell into. And, you see, sir, that's life—I don't know what happened, if someone who was here said something or wrote something somewhere, but the thing is, one day the noose didn't seem as tight as before, the path had been cleared. Nobody came to annoy us anymore; we suspected something worse might fall on our heads after that period of calm. But weeks went by and no news; our persecution by the Deputy and the law clerk became a thing of the past. In order to be sure, we made some careful inquiries. Not a trace: it seemed like the earth had swallowed them. Just three or four months later, we were able to find something out, but if you have no objection, I'll tell you about it in a little while.

"We gradually went back to our routine, trying to repair the damage of those past months, and then a plague that was even worse attacked us: time, sir, and sickness. Señor Ferrari always said that life is a series of waves, and that we float on top; each wave carries us out a little farther and leaves us on top of the next one, which is always rougher than the last, especially in old age; and that's how it is till you reach the last little wave, the last goodbye. And I, for one, can prove that it's true, that the guy knew what he was talking about. Because no sooner were we saved from the Deputy wave than we were carried off by the wave of sickness. First came Rick: one night he complained of something like cloudiness in his eyes, and the next day he could hardly see at all. We took him to the eye doctor, we spent money we didn't have, and the only thing we got out of it was the name of what was wrong with him, which, by the way, I can't remember. After that, his hearing got worse and worse, and he had weakness in his legs; we had to adapt his scenes so he could keep acting in them. Then, very, very quickly, Elsa: one afternoon she slipped and broke I don't know how many bones. She had to spend quite a while in bed in a cast. Then, when our medical expenses were driving us crazy, Renault started having more serious problems with cramps; the alcohol and camphor rubs didn't help him anymore; now he needed a doctor, injections. And the people, the public, I mean, grew less and less. One day we raised the white flag, like they say, and decided to cut our losses, to cut expenses. The medications were the most important thing, so we had to sacrifice a few little things; electricity, for example, which took up a large fraction of our take. We thought these lanterns and candles would give Casablanca a touch of mystery, and would save us a few pesos in the process. Luckily, people liked it from the beginning; they even thought it had always been like that ('a country-style Casablanca,' they said, not realizing what this had been like before). Then we changed the way we charged. Before, we used to collect a set fee which included a drink (when Señor Ferrari was alive, there was no need for a cover charge; people would uncork bottle after bottle of champagne, and even the most uneducated customers would order caviar); but now we thought it would be better not to charge and give each person the freedom to put whatever he thought we deserved in that jar, that one over there. Because, as one of us said, in the past we used to offer just a show, but now, I also tell our story, and so there's sort of an added value, right? Rick's here, Elsa's here, I'm here, we've got music, and if that's not enough, we've also got the story of Casablanca, each day and each character. The good and the bad that all these years have brought us. *Our* movie, what came afterward, and the present. What do you say, sir? Are we right or not?"

I thought he was asking a rhetorical question, but he stopped, waiting for me to respond. His last few words didn't have the same force as a while earlier; even his gaze had lost its intensity. I thought he was trying to gloss over the details, to hurry, like someone who's approaching the end of something and can no longer stand being separated from it. I also imagined he was tired, and felt something like pity for him, for his comrades, and for everything in that place. Nevertheless, I didn't let any of these thoughts show, but rather replied with an affirmative nod and a look that was intended to encourage him to continue, as though he had just begun the story.

"Because, sir," he went on, a bit more animated, "it's not a question of a few more pesos; it's a question of recognition. Look, the business with the law clerk and the Deputy (to continue with what I promised you a few minutes ago) hurt us so badly because they were playing with those very feelings;

they didn't realize they would lose everything that way. But, of course, in that case it was a question of criminals with no appreciation for art, for the efforts of an artist, a visionary. And luckily, one of them, the Deputy, got what was coming to him. Like I told you, we thought he had let up on us because he was tired or because someone had taken our side without saying anything to us. But later we discovered that just a little while after he stuck his nose in our business, the Deputy was thrown out of Parliament for corruption; he had tried to extort money from a chicken farmer who was out of compliance. And the other guy, the law clerk, learned his lesson right away; a few days after the business with the Deputy (we didn't know anything about it yet), he sent us a message telling us he had thought it over, that we were right for acting as we did, and that he wanted to apologize in person. Nobody here wanted to let him come, but I ended up meeting with him in the doorway for a while. He didn't say a word about the Deputy's fall, but rather he tried to make me believe he was truly sorry and that he had separated from the other guy just like that, because he was a better person. I let him talk, and he left convinced I had swallowed his story. We know we still have to be careful with him, but so far, nothing unusual has happened.

"So, sir, that's how we've spent the last three or four years, with no big changes. Without slacking off, always ready to serve our public, to show them what this is. In winter and in summer, rain or shine. Because you probably noticed how we received you with our curtains wide open, like they say in the theater. The reason the chairs are all stacked up there is to keep the wind from blowing out the candles if someone comes in. And Rick . . . well, sometimes he has days when he's dead tired and not even the pills can help him shake it. But, for sure, no matter what, Casablanca showed its colors today, storm or no storm . . . which looks like it's over, by the way; at least, I don't hear the rain anymore."

He grew quiet, stood up wearily and began sweeping the room with his gaze. I stood up, too, and did the same.

"Casablanca . . . Casablanca . . ." he said a moment later, as if thinking aloud. "Who knows . . . of the many people who've passed through here, seeing and listening to me . . . maybe one of them will decide to write its story. Or maybe they've already written it; who can tell? If so, it wouldn't matter if the story's not up to date, if they only talk about a performance from long ago. The important thing is for it to be told, to be written. That would be wonderful; then it really wouldn't matter what came next, wind or water . . ."

He sighed deeply and remained silent, staring toward the entrance, his way of saying that the "show" had ended. I did the same (my way of establishing a transition), and very soon the story he had told me began to lose its reality and dissolve in a realm like that of dreams unraveling, when they abandon their fullness a moment before we awaken. Brusquely, I thought that if Elsa, who had impressed me so greatly a moment before, were to come back in, I might be able to see right through her body; its consistency wouldn't be unlike a ghost's. Rick, the phony Rick himself, whose table I was facing, would appear to me like a shadow at the instant it's vaporized by a beam of light, removing all possibility of identity. Only the black man . . . only Sam still emitted a certain aura of vigilance, so to speak, as if his silhouette were a kind of signpost for me, placed there to unite and sustain that symphony of phantoms. Suddenly, without realizing exactly what I was doing, I began to walk toward the front door. I felt like I was surrounded by ghosts, and I wanted to get out of there. But just then a voice detained me: "Sir . . ."

I stopped, immediately recovering my sense of reality. I turned slowly. Sam had his hands clasped at his waist, his eyes lowered.

"Sir, please . . ." he repeated, without changing posture, seeing that I hadn't caught on at all. A glass jar, on the bar, drew my attention. I vaguely understood that I was supposed to remember something. Sam cleared his throat, and then I reacted.

"Excuse me, please. Please," I said, digging my hand into my pocket. I pulled out a handful of bills and went to place them in the jar; then I searched my other pockets, managing to add a bit more, including a few coins. He held that position of ceremonious gravity, aware of everything.

"Thank you very much. Thank you," I said, passing alongside him.

I walked down the hall with long strides. I don't know why I didn't want to run into anyone else from that place. Before I reached the pile of chairs, the piano began playing:

You must remember this
A kiss is . . .

The voice became lost behind me. I crossed the threshold (one of the double doors was half-open) and received a gust of wind in my face. It was no longer raining, and the sky was starting to clear up. I considered stopping a moment to take notice of the architecture of the place, its details. But I didn't; I had the sudden sensation that everything was miraculously built on quicksand, and I was afraid I wouldn't be able to get out. I skimmed over a few puddles and got into my car. When I turned on the headlights, a confusion of structures seemed to surround me. I maneuvered, trying to avoid the water-filled potholes, and something moved in my rear-view mirror; lighting his way with a kerosene lantern, a man in a white uniform approached with the boy. I completed the maneuver and drove forward along the path. The man (Renault) and the boy stopped to watch me drive off. I noticed (or imagined) the man's surprised expression at my departure.

I went out to the main road with the feeling of having spent an infinite time in that place, as if the film had developed before me from its début performance, but with a slight change of detail. An infinite film, like the answer to the ever-repeated questions of viewers new and old; in that place, among those walls and decorations, the only possible continuation of the film had taken root, its authentic sequel; celluloid yielding to reality. A ramification, really—I thought as the air coming in through the car window freed me of something very much like vertigo—a ramification of the original story that, without departing from it entirely, brought it back, elevating it with the shimmer of nuance born of its contact with life. And this imitation of some characters' actions, all the while offering the dailiness of their lives to time, was the greatest distinction and the only legitimacy of a group of individuals who had been brought together by a whim. In a forgotten corner of the Argentine countryside, without seeking it and quite possibly without knowing it, they had managed to transcend their condition of mere reflections; their diligence and dedication had returned them to the dramatized origins. Surmounting the flow of fantasy, they had become—they *were* Rick, Ilsa, Ugarte, Strasser. For that very reason—I thought, speeding down the road that now seemed like the aisle of a movie theater at the end of a film—for that very reason, whether or not Sam's desire was fulfilled (perhaps someone will take up his story one day), neither water nor wind will ever be able to erase the Casablanca they brought to life.

Translated by Andrea G. Labinger

The Journey

Etonnant voyageurs!
—Baudelaire. *Le voyage,* III

At the hour when night seems to gather in its tapestries to the tinkling of frozen crystal, and the weakest of the stars throw themselves toward the still-darkened earth, terrified by the imminent catastrophe of daybreak, at that hour, propitious for the plotting of outrageous things and for the bubbling up of fantasy, precisely at that moment, the brief tolling of a bell, sterile and seemingly veiled in cobwebs, shook the sleeping town. Just when the familiar silence of the ordinary is about to return, another peal, equally brief, rouses the sleepers, whose drowsy attention is immediately solicited by two or three additional tollings that seem to be testing the metal integrity of the bell. But after another especially intense stroke of the clapper, followed by others in hurried succession, the bell emits a high-pitched and continuous boom that, turning its sound waves into a lengthened serpent, begins first to course through the town's streets with implacable sinuosity, and then, by means of its necessary and repeated forkings, assaults the doors, rattles the windows and, slipping through cracks, draws out into the streets with the furor of a wartime levy the amazed occupants who do not yet understand but nonetheless cannot ignore the irresistible command, of the bell that back at the station continues to toll.

It takes only a moment for the main street, which has slightly tilted so as to facilitate the procession, to overflow with the growing hubbub of the crowd advancing, at different paces, toward the station. To be sure, the procession is disorderly. The children run ahead screeching and swerving from one side of the street to the other; some women carry their dogs in their arms; others drag suitcases behind them, sidestepping the perplexed people who, falling back, are muttering curses. Occasionally, someone turns around, as if to determine if he is the only person responding to the call; he disappears immediately, swallowed up by the multitude that is frantically pushing ahead amid clouds of dust.

Finally, the mob, gasping with astonishment, stops in front of the station. There, straddling the rusty rails, dark and shining, a locomotive trembles impatiently, trying to communicate with snorts and whistles and vibrating connecting rods its eagerness to depart. The coaches, that stretch along the entire length of the platform, are also straining and their bright metal surfaces dazzle the sleepy crowd that can do nothing but stare.

After a moment, the most intrepid of the group climb up the boarding stairs to take a look at the inside of the coaches, which, to judge from their shouts, are empty. Suddenly, a cry of surprise greets the appearance, on top of the locomotive, of the engineer, a man of rosy complexion with a long mustache, whose chubby hands are stroking constantly at his blue uniform. From his vantage point he greets the crowd with broad gestures and then, with a playful smile, pulls a lever releasing a thick cloud of smoke that rises several feet in the air and then suddenly, just as the smoke is about to assume the shape of a genie or some such creature, it drops onto the people below, who run off in terror in all directions. But it is merely a joke, a frightening specter made of smoke that promptly dissipates to the amusement of the engineer as well as the relieved townspeople, who nonetheless immediately back off again, since next to the engineer, amid traces of smoke, as if emerging from a swamp, has begun to appear the figure of the fireman, whose presence, once he has risen to his full height, draws an exclamation of fright from the crowd. And in fact his appearance is frightening: extraordinarily tall, a true titan, his muscular body strains at his tight-fitting clothes, which are completely covered with soot, as is his enormous head, crowned with kinky hair that looks like a spider's nest. His face, dark and shiny, is fixed in an evil grin, calculated and self-sure, in whose presence each person feels himself confronted with an old, uncertain fear.

Placing his claw-like hands on the side of the engine, the engineer looks down at the crowd, which continues to move back. Suddenly, he whispers something to the engineer, who nods and turns away. Another cloud of smoke billows out from the smokestack, but the crowd, alerted to the trick, pays no attention and simply continues observing the stoker, who, annoyed at the failure of his joke, disappears inside the locomotive.

In the meantime, the smoke has begun to change into a kind of fog that, while it lends a fantastic aura to the place, also gives it an air of importance, making it appear somehow like the train stations of great cities, where imposing men in trench coats bid farewell to their lovers or, silhouetted against a curtain of mist, await the secret password of a fugitive. Of course, this impression lasts only a moment, since the milling about of the future travelers, their jockeying for position, the darting about of little children and the last-minute concerns about things left behind, all prevent the creation of the low, impersonal murmur of a large city's train station, which is so appropriate to more sophisticated settings. A guard, whom no one has seen until that moment, suddenly appears on the platform, clapping his hands and announcing the train's departure; arriving alongside the locomotive, he signals to the engineer. Immediately, a whistle sounds, whose increasing shrillness not only causes the fog, whipped into a whirling cloud, to be pulled back into the smokestack, but also as it disappears has drawn all of the passengers into their seats. So it is that when it ceases, everyone is aboard, and even the people who a short time before were seeing their friends onto the train now find that they themselves are among the passengers. After having accommodated their baggage in the overhead racks, the travelers spend time delightedly examining their seats, the walls, the ceiling, decorated with an eye for warmth and intimacy, and no matter where one sits, the luxury and the views are magnificent; every seat is the best seat.

The platform is now deserted and everyone is awaiting the signal to depart. Nervously, the passengers peer out of the windows, trying to determine the reason for the delay; but no one is on hand to offer an explanation. The whole town is deserted and the only thing to be heard is the throbbing of the engine. Attached to a wooden crossbar, the solitary bell sways gently. The travelers are seized with panic and questions arise. What if someone appears to announce that the journey is suspended, that it was all an absurd mistake . . . ? But then a mood of calm expectancy quiets them, like that which precedes some extraordinary event. At that moment a single ray of sunshine, after reflecting off the metallic surfaces of the train, strikes the little bell, which begins to ring merrily (Who rang the bell? *God,* an old woman replies), thus indicating the train's departure and receiving the reply of a long whistle from the engine. At the same moment, without the passengers being aware of it in the midst of their wild cheering, something astonishing happens: a tremor shakes the earth and the worm-eaten sleepers, that have barely sustained the weight of the rails and the train, seem to bring forth new life, since a great outflowing of sap, issuing from the ground itself, rejuvenates and strengthens them; the moss that has grown over the rails now begins to crumble away and the resulting fragments turn into patches of spongy flannel that an invisible hand rubs over the metal; and then, a little farther on, emerging from a long arthritic sleep, the switch point levers creak in gratitude for the welcome dew that flows like an oily elixir through their rusty and creaking joints. The engine driver, taking note of this sudden metamorphosis, leans out of his cab and makes a signal with his arm; in the distance someone replies to him with the same sign. All of this seems to indicate that everything is in order, in compliance with regulations, so that the time has come for departure.

And so it is: amid shouts, the waving of arms, the barking of dogs, endless joyful embraces, the handsome train at last draws away from the abandoned station and, advancing over a field of clover split by rails, the train, with an eager pawing of its wheels, lunges forward into the mysterious iridescence of the wondrous . . .

I I

Steadily and joyfully, the train cleaves through space and at the same time seems to slice through the earth, since in its wake the greenery that flanks the rails gives off, like contented sighs, the gentle aromas of something newborn. And inside the coaches, surrounded by metal and silk, the passengers surrender to the pleasures of simple contemplation. Nowhere is there uttered a word of displeasure, not even a question, nothing. Everything about them is trusting and peaceful, relaxed and confident. The landscape, the train, the allayed concerns, all of this is for each passenger like the scent of an invisible flower, completely unquestioned and sufficient in itself to be recognized.

. . . And the countryside sways with the twists and turns of a capricious perspective that at times pierce the eyes with sharp points and angles and at other times draw the gaze gently through the flowing path of a spiral that extends its circles off into infinity.

. . . And the eagerness of the glances seems to center itself on sharp points that penetrate everything, digging up, lifting, so that every detail of the landscape is included in a kind of immensely acceptable act of plundering. Yes, the surveying gazes of the passengers is inexorable and no feature escapes examination.

At times, a perfectly simple, or common, image is offered to a passenger's eye with the full dimension of a carving, so that for a while he can observe a man throwing his hat into the air or a young woman bending over to pick vegetables or a cow standing like a sentinel under a solitary tree or, cast over the dew-covered grass, the precise shadow of a woodpecker. The image is then diffused into a faint mist out from which the traveler emerges with the sense of his vision having been cleansed.

. . . And when the passengers pass quickly past a station platform filled with people who are signaling to the train to stop, the "no, no, no" communicated by their waggling fingers is less a mockery than a sign of confidence in their having been selected as the chosen ones.

. . . And when darkness falls the passengers settle down, surfeited, and gazing up at the moon they offer a prayer of thanks for that day and for the new and extraordinary experiences that, rolled up in the dark parchment of the night, await them on the following day.

. . . And beyond every clearing in the woods that stretch along the tracks, always, like a friendly and vigilant eye, a fleeting view of the sea.

. . . And the seasons come and recede gently, seemingly on tip-toe, as if nature wanted to blend her flowerings and witherings into a softly glowing totality of regal splendor.

. . . A passenger with deep-set eyes and a long beard carries with him a blue-covered notebook into which he writes down impressions of the trip, while in the margins he tries to capture with artless strokes certain details of the landscapes he has seen. Occasionally, his traveling companions ask him to read a paragraph or two and attentively, quite impressed, they hear the words that describe what they themselves have seen or felt, and that now, transformed into literary expression, seems irreconcilable, distant, like something belonging to legend, something with a flavor in which it is now possible to detect the fine dust of decrepitude.

. . . And for moments the passengers think they feel upon them a slight, subtle pressure—something similar to the weight of a gaze.

III

Thus, in a mood of satisfaction and complacency, without pauses or stops for boarding, the blessed journey continues. One day, however, something astonishing occurs: a child predicts—and accurately—the appearance of a specific feature of the countryside. When he is questioned, he replies that all he did was remember the places that he had already seen, some of which apparently have begun to be repeated, as if movement was being reversed. Alarmed, the passengers crowd to the windows and with narrowing glances examine the countryside. *There!* shouts someone, pointing toward a distant mountain outcropping. Several travelers recognize it and now conjectures arise over what will be waiting for them farther on.

At the outset, the predictions do not coincide very closely with reality, but then, slowly, the correct guesses begin accumulating, to the point that it is no longer possible to have any doubt: even as the train continues forward, it is actually making the return trip. In some place, at some moment, the fatal turnoff occurred, but no one took notice; and now the train is going back. An anguished cry fills the coaches and immediately all the voices merge into one single plea: *Turn back!* But it is useless, the clamor scarcely reaches the interior of the locomotive, where the stoker, his teeth clenched, his gaze fixed, seems to have become intoxicated with his increasingly furious shoveling of coal. The most excited passengers cry out for a storming of the locomotive and the subduing of its occupants; but the mention of the terrifying stoker leaves them all paralyzed. Yet others, seized by an irresistible compulsion, throw themselves from the train and their bodies disappear into the brush. The women weep and hug their children, who, seeing their mothers' desperation, let out squeals that blend in with the curses of the men. So it is that, to the accompaniment of writhing bodies, distorted expressions, and arms extended out toward the direction from which they came, it begins to grow dark and the train now penetrates the night like a long lament.

Daybreak finds the travelers awake and stiff-jointed. They have not slept during the night and they are exhausted. Some seats are now vacant. A child is calling out for its mother; a woman searches, sobbing, for her husband. Some passengers remain with their heads leaning on the sills of the window frames, indifferent to the leaves and branches that whip across their faces. No one listens to those who are still stubbornly encouraging hope or patience;

these passengers, feeling too deceived to be consoled with words, prefer silence.

Outside, the land is no longer bright; obscured by a cloud of ashes from
some unknown incinerated region, it receives the spiteful gazes of the passengers, who now repeatedly discover, beneath the hovering overcast, certain
features of the landscape that they recall. But their attitude is not betrayed by
any outward gesture; deprived of the discovery of new sights, they immerse
themselves in a feigned indifference, the same as that they will maintain, like
some sort of valuable benefit, for the rest of the journey, which, in a certain
sense, could be said to be starting over . . .

I V

. . . And, slumped in their hard seats, the travelers indulge in a fitful exchange
of recollections, that surface like so many threads turned up after lengthy
digging into memories. Not even the children retain from the journey (*The
journey out* as they refer to it in subdued voices) anything more than a series
of sensations that are impossible to express.

. . . And the arguments and the disturbances are not long in appearing.
A woman in a torn dress flees to another coach, pursued by a man; a child
strikes his brother who refuses to give him the butterfly he has just caught.

. . . And progressively the colors outside fade, and a shadowy cloud, speck-
led with black dots, settles over the countryside. A passenger looks out and
points up toward something; up above, a huge gray cloud, its center radiant
with sunlight, spills out from its sides, like an enormous candle, a faint drizzle
of ash-colored light.

. . . And every detail of the landscape, every sound or word casually heard,
evokes in each passenger the insipid daily routine of life before, whose symbols and crosses are seen through memory as increasingly terrible, like the
signs pointing out an infernal trajectory.

. . . Some desperate persons seize the blue notebook from the hands of its
owner and frantically read its pages out loud. But the words sound strange,
meaningless. They are pure sound, and the sketches that accompany that
linguistic mishmash appear to the person looking at them, who in turn passes
the notebook to other avid hands, like the tracks of a sprawling insect. In a

corner a man with a long beard bundles himself up in his coat and turns his gaze to the window.

. . . And the train resembles more and more the empty shell of a long-dead beetle, but one in whose interior there still swarm, blind and powerless, a cluster of larvae . . .

V

Then one night, on rounding a curve, the small abandoned train station appears. The train pulls up gently in front of the stationmaster's office. On the surface of the coaches, moistened with dew, the diminutive stars are reflected. The moon emerges from among the clouds and in the distance the little group of houses is bathed in white light, like a cemetery. The sudden silence awakens the travelers, who immediately recognize where they are. Slowly, now older, they descend with difficulty from the train and gather together in front of the wooden station house. They seem confused and their meek expressions are fixed on the ground. Finally, an old man looks up at the stars, as if to get his bearings, and then begins walking slowly toward the town, followed by the rest of the travelers.

They move ahead, dragging their feet, their joints creaking. There are now only a few people left on the platform. One of them, bringing up the rear, looks at the old bell; then he approaches it and his hands grasp the frayed rope. He waits for the last of the travelers to leave the station and then gives a tug on the rope. A deep, muffled sound reverberates from the metal of the bell. The man sighs and pulls once again on the rope. This time the sound reaches the group of travelers who are moving down the road and they stop to listen to it. Another peal of the bell causes them to pause and they lift their trembling hands to their heads, as if trying to extract a memory. But now the shrill peals begin to accumulate and each one of them sounds like the lash of a whip in the ears of the travelers who, spurred on by the tolling, hasten their steps.

But they can proceed only a short distance because in front of them there is advancing a huge cloud of dust, noisy and terrifying, accompanied by the sound of hurried footsteps. The foremost part of the cloud now reaches the front ranks of the frightened travelers, who remain there in the middle of

the road, fascinated by the tolling bell and by the dust cloud, which continues advancing relentlessly. They need to stand aside, as their coughing
and complaints now require, and yet they do not budge from their position.
Something new freezes them in place: the sudden conviction of an imminent
remembrance, with which perhaps . . . But no, there is no longer time; the
cloud of dust now envelops them, and their consciousness is overcome. . . .

Translated by D.A.Y.

❧ *The Siesta*

Seated on the dirt floor, the young boy wiped away the saliva from his lips and looked up at his grandfather, who was dozing in a hammock chair facing the doorway. The sounds of the clucking hens in the back yard and the rattle of the dishes that his grandmother was washing in the next room were clearly carried on the hot, humid air. The noise and the heat easily penetrated into the room through the loosely fitted slats of the door, making the old man's slumber seem imperturbable. The boy decided to try raising his voice a little.

"Grampa, tell me where you put the ball. Can you hear me, Grampa?" he repeated wearily, his gaze cast down on the stick he was using to dig at the earthen floor.

A deep sigh was the only response from the grandfather, who finally relaxed completely as his head tilted forward.

"Don't make me think you're sleeping, Grampa," the boy said in his louder voice as he reached toward the chair.

But unexpectedly the door opened and the sudden light forced him to close his eyes.

"Don't bother your grandfather. Let him sleep," his grandmother said softly as she walked past him. She went over to a mirrored closet door next to the metal-frame bed, which was where the child slept at night.

The boy lowered his head and kept on digging.

The woman took an armful of clothing from the closet and turned back. The light from the hallway filtered in through the half-open door and outlined the figures of the old man and the boy. The season of most oppressive heat had not yet arrived, but the woman's husband had already sought out the coolness of that mud-walled, thatch-roofed room at the back of the house next to the kitchen. The siesta was in part a compensation for his nights of unrelenting insomnia. There was a slight movement from the man in the chair and the boy began digging with more determination.

The woman leaned back against the closet door and looked down at the boy. He sensed her gaze and moved his body slightly, hiding from her view the pile of dirt that he had dug up. The woman smiled tenderly and experienced again the things she felt whenever her attention lingered on him—pity, sympathy. Less on the child's account, in truth, than for herself and her husband. This was their grandson, a creature with teary eyes who still soiled himself and had saliva constantly forming at the corners of his mouth. A kind of animal almost, the product of the whim of a passing stranger and the fear of spinsterhood of a simple country girl, her daughter. What is more, a daughter from whom they had heard nothing for years until she suddenly reappeared to leave with them the fatherless child, which no school would ever accept.

Her feeling of pity increased, now concentrated completely on the child. She felt the urge to take him into her arms and console him for the misfortune that his limited intelligence probably could not perceive. But she did not. That noon the boy had broken a flower vase with his ball and she and her husband had agreed to express their anger toward him at least until supper and then, as on so many other occasions, they would find a way to forgive him for his misdeed. She pressed the armful of clothes to her breast and went to the door.

"Gramma, please. My ball," a plaintive voice begged as she moved past the chair.

The woman turned, observed him for a moment and only with great effort gave him a silent reproving look, warning him to be quiet, as she left the room.

When the sound of her footsteps died out at the far end of the hall, the child looked at his grandfather. A gentle snore was escaping from his half-opened mouth.

"Grampa," he insisted, in a drawn-out voice, his eyes fixed on the floor, "the ball. I want my ball, Grampa."

Silence.

The child paused for a moment while he sank nearly half the length of his stick into the ground. Then, while he struggled to sink the stick even further into the earth, he said in a soft voice: "If you won't give me the ball, will you tell me a story? Did you hear me, Grampa?"

The old man breathed heavily through his mouth, half-opened his eyes, coughed, and then fell back to sleep.

"Grampa?" the boy insisted hopefully, because on other occasions his grandfather had pretended to be asleep and the boy had discovered the deception.

But this time the fixed expression on the sleeping man's face caused him to back down. He shifted his legs to one side and went back to playing with the stick.

Another long silence was marked only by the song of an oven bird somewhere outside that announced its arrival with fluttering and chirping. The child observed the fragmented shadow of the bird through the vertical cracks in the door, then looked back at his grandfather.

"Grampa, you didn't tell me a story today," the boy persisted, but without raising his voice. "Before taking your nap, you have to tell me a story. You know that, Grampa."

The old man seemed for a moment to be chewing on something, then went on breathing through his mouth.

"The story about the lady and the bag, Grampa," he begged, encouraged by the movement of his grandfather's mouth. "Go ahead, Grampa. The story about the lady and the bag, when you were a policeman," he said as he settled down at the foot of the chair.

Of all the stories that—unbeknownst to his wife—the grandfather would tell him before the siesta (all going back to the time when he was a police constable in the small town), this was the boy's favorite. He never tired of hearing it, even though he knew it by memory, because the old man had repeatedly resorted to it to insure that some act of mischief wouldn't interrupt his afternoon rest.

The boy waited at the foot of the chair, his gaze fixed on his grandfather. Then he slowly returned to the spot where he had been seated before.

"All right, Grampa," he said in a less aggressive tone, as he resumed his game with the stick. "If you don't want to tell me, it doesn't make any difference. I remember it. I don't need you. I'll tell it myself. Did you hear?"

He paused to see what his grandfather's reaction would be. Then, since there was none, he lowered his head and began to speak.

"It was a long time ago. I was . . . by then a constable," he said and then stopped to glance up. "A child, a baby had been stolen," he continued, now with a defiant edge to his voice, moving his gaze back and forth between his grandfather and the earthen floor, "and nobody had any leads. The baby's parents were out of their minds with worry. The chief of police called me in and said that I . . . I had to do the investigation and find out where they had hidden the baby. And so, well, I began to look into it."

The boy's speech abruptly broke off, but his lips continued forming words. Then, just as suddenly, his voice returned, but only for a few seconds. Now he began alternating speech with silent pauses, looking for some response from his grandfather.

"It turned out to be a couple of drifters, homeless scum who lived in the streets." A glance. No response. He continued. "We really gave it good to these bums, but we learned nothing. I was beginning to get nervous, the chief was putting pressure on me . . . On one of them I came across a scrap of paper with the name of a woman on it. Martha something or other. She must have had the baby. We found her but not the baby. We didn't hold back anything . . . she was crying all the time, but even when we slapped her good with a damp towel, she wouldn't talk. So then I said to her, "All right, now I know a way to really make you spill what you know . . .""

The child suddenly fell silent and looked up at his grandfather, who was snoring peacefully. He got up and went to the door and looked out through the crack. There was no one outside. He glanced back at his grandfather with a pensive, uneasy expression. Then he quietly opened the door and stepped into the hall. The bright light blinded him for a moment. When his eyes adjusted, he went down the hall to the kitchen, where the door stood half open. He glanced inside and looked around the room that his grandmother had tidied up, then went in. He stopped at the kitchen table and picked up from a napkin-covered bread basket a scrap of bread left over from lunch. Eating it, he went to the window that looked out into the patio, where some sparrows were competing with the chickens for a few pieces of watermelon rind. He turned and went back to the table where he paused, as if he had forgotten why he had gone into the kitchen.

"All right, now I know a way to really make you spill what you know," he repeated in his story-telling voice and went to one of the cupboards. Opening a door, he took out a green plastic garbage bag. He folded it up so that he could hide it in the small pocket of his shirt. Then, smiling excitedly, he went into the hall. The light dazzled him again. He covered his eyes and returned to the doorway. He stopped in front of the door, wolfed down the rest of the bread, and went in.

His grandfather was still sleeping, with his head now tilted over to one side. He closed the door noiselessly and waited for his eyes to adjust to the dim light. Then he went behind the chair, removed the garbage bag and unfolded it. The old man's head was motionless; only his chest and stomach moved with his respiration. He opened the bag and held it up over the back of the chair and then, biting his lips and licking the saliva around his mouth, he began to cover the old man's head. When he had it lowered all the way down over his grandfather's body, he flattened the edges out against his back and his chest. Finally, seeing that everything was set up right, he stepped back a few feet and, in a drawn-out voice, said:

"Grampa. Now you're going to have to stop pretending that you're asleep and tell me where the ball is. You've got to confess, Grampa."

And he crossed his arms and waited.

After a few moments he said: "Grampa, if you don't confess, I'm not taking the bag off. Understand?"

The grandfather's breathing started to become more labored.

"Well, Grampa, are you going to confess?" the boy said calmly.

The old man's head moved to an upright position and the edge of the bag separated from his body. The boy saw this and with a few gentle pats he flattened it out once again. Then he stepped back and crossed his arms once again.

"Grampa, I'm not in a hurry," he said in an unruffled tone after several moments had passed. To demonstrate this he went over to the mirror on the wardrobe door and looked at himself. His gaze shifted now and then back to the reflection of his grandfather. The old man was breathing with increasing difficulty, because the plastic bag had adhered to his sweat-covered neck and had shut off the passage of air. Suddenly, one of his hands raised and the plastic was noisily sucked into his open mouth. The boy noted this and believed that, as had happened with the woman in the story, his grandfather was beginning to struggle to find the air that he desperately needed. And it was after this frantic effort that, as his grandfather had told him, that the confession came. For this reason he waited where he stood for the moment to arrive when his grandfather would confess. He even urged him on with words he remembered from the story.

"Are you going to confess or do you want to suffocate?" he asked sharply, imitating the angry tone of voice that his grandfather used when he got to that part.

But the old man, it seemed, was hanging on. His hand had reached only as far as his neck, where it had come to rest, while the sound of his breathing had almost ceased.

The boy waited a few minutes in silence, surprised by his grandfather's power of resistance. Then finally, when silence fell, he moved away from the mirror and cautiously approached the chair. He stood before it, his eyes downcast, and flattened down the pile of dirt that he had dug up. Then he looked up at his grandfather.

He was amused at first by the way that the bag had adhered to his face. With his mouth and nostrils sealed by the green plastic, he seemed to be wearing a mask. Then he had a disturbing thought: it seemed that all he had managed to do was to put his grandfather really to sleep. Now he'd surely not listen to him. He gazed at the old man for a moment, with no idea of what to do. There was no movement now of his chest or his stomach and his motionless hand rested on the lower edge of the bag. Some of the white of his eyes showed through the plastic. They were half open, the way they often were when his grandfather was sleeping very soundly.

He moved now, annoyed, and reached out to remove the bag. But at that moment he heard someone approaching.

"Niki," his grandmother called out to him softly from the hallway.

Startled, the boy stepped back a few steps, still staring at his grandfather.

"Niki, the ball," the woman said in a confiding tone, opening the door part way.

On hearing that word, the grandfather's image was immediately erased from his sight. He rushed to the door and went out into the hall. His grandmother was waiting for him there. One hand was behind her back and with the other she motioned to him to be quiet. The boy approached her slowly, his gaze downcast.

"Will you promise that from now on you'll do what I tell you? Promise?" she asked as he stood before her.

Overcome with excitement, the child mumbled a few words and reached out to embrace his grandmother who now offered him the ball. He took it in his hands and did a little dance around her as she looked at him happily.

"Now go quietly and get a plastic bag from the kitchen. We have to do some weeding in the flower bed out front," the woman said and turned to go out the front door.

"Oh, yes! Yes, Gramma!" the boy exclaimed, still overjoyed at recovering his ball.

He ran to the kitchen and went to the cupboard door. But he stopped short when he opened it. He muttered something unintelligible, went back into the hall and, hushing himself with a finger raised to his lips, he approached the room where his grandfather was. He pushed the door open slowly and looked in. The old man remained in the same position. He tiptoed in and, placing the ball between his knees, began to pull off the green bag. When he removed it, he carefully smoothed out his grandfather's hair, which had become disarranged, and, after placing a few gentle kisses on his forehead, said:

"Just go on sleeping, Grampa. Don't wake up, all right. We have some work to do."

And he went out.

Translated by D.A.Y.

❧ *The Forgotten God*

There are four legends concerning Prometheus . . . According to the third, his treachery was forgotten in the course of thousands of years, forgotten by the gods, the eagles, forgotten by himself.
—Kafka, *Prometheus*

There were no longer wounds, nor eagles, nor chains. The rock had dissolved into thin air.

The light was gone and no sound could be heard. But within the perfection of that emptiness, isolated like a germ, a consciousness throbbed.

It was a fragile movement, a readjustment amid that timeless lethargy. The faint perception of something located outside time but that nevertheless seemed immersed in it, that in some way had always been there . . . But nothing definite could yet be sensed. It was only the delicate impression of a stirring, of a quivering, communicated by some kind of shallow wave that flowed inward, breaking, exhausted and meticulous, in the very center of that still unknowing conscience.

But then, suddenly, perception broadened and something approaching an understanding occurred. The quivering increased and amid the mists of lethargy there appeared several tatters of light. The understanding was becoming clearer. And anxiety emerged.

Anxiety over what was imminent, over what, becoming complete, is a beginning. A limitless anxiety as the consequence of understanding, which signaled that something was approaching. Something resembling a stronger consciousness that invaded the other consciousness and carried with it a sensation and the shred of a memory. The feeling of a softly wrinkled hollowness. The memory of shadowy beating wings and of the creak of rusted metal.

56

A recognition occurred. And quickly sorrow overwhelmed the conscious-ness. An anguished sorrow, at once sharp and muted. A frenzy of uneven stabbing pains that, probing the deepest reaches, left behind the impression of a loss, of an irremediable plundering.

For a moment, there was nothing but this rising tide of sorrow. But then, slowly, its initial strength diminished, the pain dissolved into mere discom-fort, as a result of which the consciousness quickly recovered the sensation of an ancient burden, composed of shrieks and oppressiveness, the memory of which began to form itself into an image that the increasing brightness of the sun was rendering transparent.

The understanding, however, was now more irrepressible. So much so that it could even overcome that circle of light—that was bent on erasing it with its soundless incandescence—and succeed in having the consciousness recognize, aided by a thread of shadow that suddenly intruded before it—that that spectral body, writhing under enormous chains, its side destroyed and bleeding, was ... Yes, it was a continuation, an extension of itself, the objecti-fied product of its perception, which came together in a vague and drifting memory that seemed to grow in the presence of that shadow that was begin-ning to rise over the bright horizon, murmuring a name: *Prometheus* ...

II

Prometheus ... Unfathomable was the world that this word evoked. An abyss of things that once happened, things that the consciousness was trying to remember.

Prometheus ... Like an enchantment, the repetition of this name drew the consciousness forward and communicated a sense of belonging ... Now the perception, the understanding were emerging from that name. Only thus was it possible to comprehend fully that rock, those chains, the wound in the side, and the alarmed shriek that seemed to emerge from the very sun itself. Only through knowing that he was Prometheus was it possible to raise him-self a bit, lift up an arm to shield his eyes from the sun and regard that man, that youth, whose form stood out, glowing and uncertain, in the bluish air.

Prometheus ... The faint voice merged with the sound of the waves be-low, which rose like a supplication up along the green and scaly flanks of the mountain. The titan lowered his arm and looked into the sky. All the while, the youth continued uttering his name. Then he came forward a few steps and grasped an outcropping of rock: from that position he continued speaking the name of the god.

The latter remained with his head raised up. Then he turned and his gaze met that of the youth and for an instant he had the impression of observing himself with the other's eyes. The youth began talking uncontrollably. But Prometheus was not listening to him: immersed in his own memories, he was searching for a moment. Finally, he discovered the protective darkness within which a grateful self had dissolved, at last forgotten. He moved forward slightly . . . up to the very edge where the pursuing anxiety and the pain began . . . He retreated immediately back into his shadowy refuge. But another urging penetrated that blessed place: the urging of a simple insistence that would not be denied . . .

He opened his eyes and looked back down. The indistinct murmur of a multitude seemed to envelop the youth, whose expression was radiant. He closed his eyes again. He was at once startled by a scream; he clenched his fists and a grimace of pain appeared on his face. A moment later he turned to the youth, who was trying to make himself understood, and signaled to him to stop speaking. He then showed him the chains. The youth's features glowed with intelligence and he abandoned his position.

He began to climb laboriously, grasping onto the rock. Prometheus urged him on wordlessly. At last he reached the side of the titan. A series of steep precipices surrounded the base of the rock. The youth stood up so that he could grasp the chains, but he stopped when he saw that Prometheus was reaching out trying to bring their arms together. Their eyes met. And even in the instant when he felt the shove, his eyes never left the gaze that accompanied him down into the abyss.

Translated by D.A.Y.

❧ *The Prisoner*

The door creaked open and two guards entered, leading a prisoner. After removing his clothes, they strapped him down on a wooden table and left. The prisoner, a middle-aged man with his hair receding at the temples, did not appear to have been beaten. He looked up at the ceiling and to the left and right with an expression of surprise, as if he had just awakened in a strange place. Suddenly, in the darkness at the far end of the room, the figure of a man in a gray smock stood up. He had been there from the first, but the prisoner had not noticed him. He raised his head to look in his direction. Then the man sat down again in the same place. He remained there for a few seconds, then removed a wrinkled rag from the pocket of his smock and smoothed it out. He approached the table and tied it around the head and through the mouth of the prisoner who saw only a vague form with the outline of what might have been a mustache moving quickly above him before it disappeared into the darkened corner. The man sat down, lit a cigarette and from there began to blow smoke toward the prisoner.

When he had finished smoking, he crushed the butt on the floor and joined his hands behind his head. The prisoner thought he heard him whistling. Then he heard the man's footsteps approaching. He turned to look at him. The man was now carrying a black bag and his head was covered by a hood that was also black. *It looks like velvet,* the prisoner thought without taking his eyes off the hood. The man placed the bag on the floor, bent over and opened it, then stood up holding an instrument that resembled a set of pincers, from whose handles there hung a long, coiled cable. He remained motionless for a moment, thoughtfully regarding the prisoner. Perspiration was trickling down his face into the creases that the gag had formed at the corners of his mouth. The man unrolled the cable and plugged it into a socket located beside the door. From the tips of the pincers came a humming sound that soon subsided. He returned to the table and placed the instrument on the prisoner's chest. An acrid smell of burnt hair filled the room. The prisoner trembled and held his breath. An intense swarming sensation spread over his breast. Suddenly, he felt something grab at his stomach and groaned in surprise. A new application, this time on a leg, made his body jerk. This was followed immediately by another, then another, then one more, in a dizzying series that disrupted the swarming sensation only to replace it with a searing pain that in seconds reached every part of his being. Rising above the pain, the prisoner opened his eyes. Like some kind of monstrous bumblebee, the man hovered over him, to the accompaniment of an intolerable buzzing sound. He shut his eyes again, dragged down into a vortex of conflicting feelings. He tried to scream, to laugh, to strike out, to strike himself. He felt himself drawn into a candescent and unbearable eternity; he felt he was falling into a void, pulled down by hooks sunk into his flesh. Then he lost contact with his body. His brain seemed to explode . . . He lost consciousness.

When he wakened, he was lying on the cot in his cell, once again dressed. He tried to sit up, but his entire body ached and he could scarcely move. He was choking with thirst; in a hoarse voice he called out for water. A short while later an unarmed guard entered the cell carrying a tray. On the floor he left a tin plate containing some kind of stew and a plastic glass filled with water. "Drink the water slowly," he said to him and went out. The prisoner crawled from the bed and grabbed the glass, drinking the contents without a pause. From his mouth came a sound that resembled that of hot coals being doused with water. He felt even thirstier. He imagined the sea, rain, the dirty water that runs along a street gutter. He tried once again to scream but he lost consciousness before he could. When he came to, night had fallen. Beneath the door there was a line of light coming from the hall. The plate and glass had been taken away. He crawled back onto the cot and lay facing the wall. He was overcome with pain and exhaustion. When the light on the hall went out, he was already asleep.

The following day he was once again taken to the same room. But this time the prisoner did not faint and it even seemed to him that the session was shorter than before. The man disconnected the pincers, laid them carefully into his bag and left. A moment later the guards appeared and untied him. The prisoner tried to dress himself but he was unable to bend one of his arms. They had to support him on both sides to return him to his cell. When they brought him food and water, he drank with more restraint, mainly to have something to accompany the stew. Afterward he lay on his back for a few minutes. He fell asleep almost against his will.

The next day the guards found him standing. With great difficulty he was able to walk to the room without help. He undressed himself and stretched out on the table. The guards exchanged a grin as they secured the straps and then left. The prisoner tried then to relax, since he had observed that there was no one in the corner. He closed his eyes, readjusted his position on the table and awaited the man's arrival, which he imagined was imminent. A lengthy period passed, however, and no one appeared. *A new kind of torture,* the prisoner thought as the wait became unbearable. Then the door abruptly opened and the guards entered. They began to untie him. One of them helped him get off the table and the other gave him his clothes. While he was getting dressed, the sound of footsteps came from the hall. The prisoner stood motionless. The pace of the steps increased and a man appeared in the doorway pulling on a smock, his head covered with a hood of what looked to be velvet. He seemed to be nervous and agitated as he entered the room. The bag he was carrying was open. He mumbled some excuse to the guards, but they were already placing the prisoner on the table again and did not respond. When they left, the man, who was now somewhat calmer, turned to the wall, removed the hood and lit a cigarette. But suddenly, after only a few puffs, he tossed the cigarette aside, replaced the hood and connected the instrument. It seemed to the prisoner that the humming was louder than on the two previous occasions. Moreover—perhaps because he understood that pain was what he was supposed to feel—he did not experience the swarming sensation of before, but instead, when the man placed the pincers on his shoulder the prisoner uttered a moan that the gag muffled somewhat. The smell of burning flesh caused a contraction deep in his throat. The man noticed the imminent consequence and moved his hand back and forth over the prisoner's face. *Thanks,* the prisoner surprised himself thinking before the pain washed away his thoughts.

When he had finished, the man himself undid the straps and helped him off the table. The guards appeared almost immediately and when they were leaving the room supporting the prisoner between them, the latter turned back toward the dark corner of the room. There, the man was smoking.

Two days went by during which the prisoner was not taken from his cell. But late on the third day he was awakened by the usual guards. As they were leaving the cell, one of them made a humorous comment on how all good things had to come to an end. His companion greeted this with a laugh and on the prisoner's face there appeared a kind of grimace, almost a forced smile of agreement.

The session was repeated without variation and this time the prisoner passed out twice. In the end, he was brought back to consciousness by the sound of the guards rapping on the door. They wanted to know if things were going to last much longer. The man motioned to them to come in and explained that he had become distracted and for that reason had lost track of time. The words came to the prisoner as if from a dream. He felt light-headed and was on the verge of vomiting. *He must have problems of some kind, maybe his family,* was the last thought on his mind before he fainted in the guards' grasp.

He awoke on his cot, aching and thirsty. He slipped to the floor and groped for the glass of water. The cell was pitch dark. He could not find either the glass or the plate. He stretched out on his back on the floor and placed the palms of his hands and the soles of his feet on the damp surface. The cold that was penetrating his body gave him the deceptive impression of relief from the thirst. He considered removing his jacket, but the fear of catching cold stopped him. He fell asleep where he lay.

During the days that followed, the routine of the sessions was interrupted. He was taken out once a day only to spend a short while in a patio where he sat in the sun. Several prisoners roamed about aimlessly there, but they were not allowed to approach each other or to speak. Some of them appeared to be foreigners. A whistle sounded to let them know it was time to return to their cells.

One morning the guards came for him. When he saw him, the guard who was fond of making jokes gave a shrug as if to indicate *Well, there's not much we can do about it.* The three of them smiled.

The prisoner walked along the hall in front of them. He remembered perfectly the route, which was circular. When he arrived at the room, the prisoner himself opened the door. The guards did not enter the room, but one of them looked in and made a questioning gesture. When he received a response, the two of them left. Everything there was the same, including the man in the corner. He stopped next to the table, unsure of what to do. He thought that he should acknowledge him somehow but did not find the words. In the corner the red tip of the cigarette glowed. When it went out, a dark form stepped forward. The black hood reminded the prisoner of figures of the Inquisition that he had seen in a book. The man was wearing a brown suit with a plaid shirt and a light blue sweater. The smock was hanging from a nail near the head of the table. For a moment the prisoner considered getting it for him, but the man was already reaching for it. So he stayed where he was, simply watching as he buttoned up the smock. When the last button was buttoned the prisoner asked the man if he should get undressed. "What do you think?" was the answer.

As he was placing his uniform on a chair, the prisoner remembered his first visit to a doctor without his mother. He was fourteen years old and then, as now, he had also lain down on his back on an examining table and then also a man had approached him with an instrument in his hands and . . .

A few slaps to his face brought him to. He was still tied to the table but now it was a man dressed in white who, as it had been when he was fourteen, was applying to his chest the familiar object whose extremes were placed in his ears. He looked around. At the door stood the two guards. Apparently the man had gone. After examining him carefully, the doctor put his stethoscope in a bag and left the room without a word. The guards undid the straps and told him to get dressed. He asked them what had happened. "You passed out," one of them said. The other guard, the wisecracking one, could not resist the urge to add, "Looks like our friend here just couldn't take it."

Several times later in the day, the outline of a face appeared at the peephole of his cell door. The prisoner noted this and understood the reason. He began feigning extreme pain, rolled his eyes and tried to drool. Evidently, no one believed his act, because the next day the guards were back at his cell. As he got up to accompany them, the prisoner noticed that one of them had been replaced. A young, red-headed, expressionless man had taken the place of the jokester. On the way to the room he asked the other guard the reason for the change. "He talked too much," was the reply he got. The prisoner smiled to himself and felt secretly pleased about the other guard's fate.

The man was waiting for him at the door to the room. He wore the hood over his head. Before they entered he led the prisoner to a window and, having him look toward the ceiling, examined his eyes carefully. He then asked him if he had fainted again. "No," the guard said. The prisoner looked at him with surprise. Apparently, they were watching him more carefully than he imagined. The man immediately dismissed the guards and gestured toward the door.

As had happened before, the man's attention wandered and not until he heard the guards rapping on the door did he stop. The prisoner, who had endured the session fairly well, stood up when the straps were loosened and looked carefully at the instrument, which the man had placed on a chair. The guards urged him to hurry up and indicated wordlessly that they found it hard to put up with the smell of burnt flesh inside the room. The prisoner smiled with a certain sense of self-satisfaction, feeling himself raised to some degree of importance by that show of weakness on the part of his custodians, and on the way back to the cell his step exceeded in briskness and spirit that of those accompanying him.

One day, when the prisoner entered the room, the guards having just departed, the man, who was standing near the head of the table, turned to him without covering his face. The sight of him had a profound effect on the prisoner. Vaguely, he had always felt that the hood must have concealed terrible, possibly monstrous features. So that now, seeing before him a face with perfectly unremarkable features, scarcely distinguished by the dark mustache, he was very much surprised. The man seemed equally surprised, but the reason was the confusion of the prisoner, who had begun to smile while his hands fidgeted nervously as if he were on the point of embracing a long-lost friend. The man lit a cigarette and went to the corner to smoke it. The hood lay on the table. The prisoner glanced from it to the man. The latter made a gesture and, as the prisoner took the black hood in his hands, explained, "My wife made it." The prisoner nodded and his fingers stroked the fabric with the delicacy of a person handling a relic. Impulsively, he placed it over his head and turned toward the man. Both of them laughed, and the prisoner laughed even louder when the man said, "You look like a monk."

The man worked without using the hood and he left his smock unbuttoned. But the prisoner noted that when the guards approached he hurriedly put the hood back on. When he was leaving the room, he glanced at the man with a smile suggesting a shared secret.

From this time on the man never used the hood during the sessions. At first, the prisoner felt elated over this expression of confidence, but then he started to become worried. *Maybe it means that they're going to kill me,* he thought, *and that's why he doesn't care if I can recognize him.* But another consideration reassured him: when the guards were present, he never left his head uncovered, and also when he was working without the hood, he would turn toward the door every now and then to make sure that no one was coming. *It's obvious that he's doing this at his own risk,* the prisoner finally decided. For his own sake, he asked the man about it. A sudden expression of displeasure that pulled up his mustache was the response. But halfway through the session the man seemed to have forgotten the matter, because he asked the prisoner, "Did you see the soccer game last night?" But he immediately corrected himself, "Oh, I forgot that you prisoners don't watch television." He fell silent and said no more. *He has talked to me a lot all at once,* the prisoner thought and looked at the man with curiosity.

Later on the sessions were reduced to three times each week. The number of guards was also cut back from two to one. The young, red-haired man had been excused for having completed his term of conscription and he was not replaced. The prisoner, in fact, did not need a guard. This also appeared to be the understanding of the authorities in charge, since one day the prisoner heard someone approach to open his door and then walk away. He waited a moment but no one appeared. He was surprised because it was a day for a scheduled session. After a while, seeing that the guard did not come to get him, he went out into the hallway, which was deserted. He stood in the doorway, thinking. Finally, he made up his mind. In a measured pace, neither hurried nor slow, he walked toward the room. Once there, he entered decisively. The man was there, waiting for him. From that day on, he made the trip to and from the room alone. When he returned to his cell, someone closed the door and slid the bolt shut. The prisoner would then stretch out on his cot, smiling with satisfaction.

The man seemed equally satisfied with the prisoner. At the latter's request, he no longer placed a gag in his mouth, so that if the pain was not unbearable, they could converse about various matters.

At times, before they began, the prisoner would comment playfully with the man about their respective moods, and if he was in good humor, the prisoner would pretend to threaten him with the pincers. The man would laugh and act as if he was frightened.

On one occasion, the man arrived carrying a small fan. The prisoner inquired repeatedly about his reason for bringing it, and he had to wait until he was strapped onto the table to find out its purpose. "A courtesy of the management," said the man as he plugged in the fan. The prisoner expressed with an exclamation his gratitude for the novelty, since the smell of burnt flesh was something that he had never become accustomed to. "No more wrinkled noses," the man responded, playing along with the prisoner's expansive attitude.

In this fashion the days passed and turned into weeks. By now the prisoner knew almost as much about the man's family as he himself did and, by virtue of certain anecdotes, he came to care deeply for its members. At times the man would bring along his daughter's workbooks so that the prisoner could correct the homework lessons that she had to take to school. On other occasions, it was a dessert prepared by his wife that the prisoner received. Some time later he asked the man if he would bring his wife and daughter to the detention center so that he could meet them. The man explained that this was impossible, and his reply left the prisoner in low spirits for several days.

One day something unusual happened. The prisoner was waiting for his door to be opened so that he could go to the room, but time passed, noon came and went, and no one appeared at the cell. The prisoner became increasingly disturbed. Then he heard the sound of footsteps. He went to the door and looked through the peephole; it was a guard bringing his meal. Excitedly, he asked why his door hadn't been opened that morning; but the guard did not know the answer. Disturbed, the prisoner hardly touched his food.

Close to dusk, he heard footsteps once again. He lay waiting on his cot. When the door opened two guards he did not know entered the cell. One of them was carrying a package; the other one gave him the news. The man had died the night before, and among his effects had been found a handwritten list of wishes that the man wanted carried out in the event that something happened to him. One of those requests, it turned out, was that the prisoner be given, as a gift and remembrance, the package that the guard was holding. That was all they could tell him. The prisoner accepted the package in silence. The guards departed, leaving the cell door open.

The prisoner waited for a moment, then began tearing off the wrapping paper and the gift was revealed. It was the black bag. After gazing at it with an indefinable expression on his face, he placed it on the edge of the cot, sat down and opened it. The black hood (looking just like velvet) was wrapped around the instrument. The prisoner removed the pincers and ran his hands slowly over them. The nickeled surface of one of the sides reflected the fragmented image of his face, and for an instant he imagined himself with a mustache. Then he replaced the instrument carefully and covered it with the hood. He noticed then that the cell door was open. He went out into the hall. There was no one there. He went back into the cell and picked up the bag. Then he went back out into the hall and began walking toward the room. He carried the bag in one hand and his firm and erect posture would have led anyone to believe that he was a member of the detention center staff.

The door of the room was open. As he entered, he had the sense that he was being observed. He placed the bag on the table and went to sit down for a moment in the darkened corner. Then he returned to the table and, opening the bag, took out the hood and the pincers. After plugging the cable into the wall socket, he laid the instrument on the table alongside the hood. He began to undress. Once he had removed his clothes, he got up onto the table and secured his feet with the straps. Before doing the same with his left hand, he placed the gag in his mouth. Then he put on the hood and picked up the instrument, which was humming softly. When he finally lay on his back on the table, he lifted the hand that held the pincers and slowly, with precision, touched it to his shoulder.

Translated by D.A.Y.

❧ The Blessing

Our Presidential residence is situated in the very center of the Capital, and two or three blocks of luxurious mansions surround it like protective rings. Continuing outward from these homes, the humbleness of the outlying dwellings accelerates at an extraordinary pace. At a distance of five blocks they are little more than shacks, and at the periphery, they are miserable hovels.

A geometric garden, dotted here and there with flower beds, encircles the central building—almost a hundred years old and ornately Italian. For some time now, the garden has attracted the gazes and murmurings of the citizens on account of a strange ceremony that unfolds on its paths each evening. What happens is that as soon as he finishes his dinner, the President goes out into the garden accompanied by an aide-de-camp who carries a silver tray with a revolver on it. When they arrive at the head of the main path, the aide-de-camp presents the tray to the President, who, in the meantime, has pulled on some silk gloves. The President takes the gun, examines it, nods in approval, and then, as he begins strolling around the grounds, fires it overhead. The pauses between one discharge and the next are regular, almost exactly timed, and the President stops only for the aide-de-camp to load the gun once its chamber has been emptied.

When the first shot rings out, the poorest people go out into the patio or porch of their homes and stay there, waiting expectantly. Those who have children, line them up on a bench and make them sit there. So as not to be late, the crippled take their places one by one a little early and ease their wait by quietly reciting certain conciliatory prayers. And after a little while, when the shooting ceases, everyone starts asking who could be the lucky one who managed to be wounded by the President . . .

And yet, it hasn't been long since the people used to tremble when the shooting began (which apparently helped the President to relax and manage

68

a good night's sleep) and no one dared to go out into the street for fear of being "blessed by the President's bullet," as they used to say jokingly. But one night, while her parents were distracted, a little girl went out onto the patio of her home, curious about the gunshots. After awhile, her mother noticed she was gone and ran out to find her. But it was too late; the little girl was lying on the ground, bleeding. She wasn't dead, however, because the bullet had only struck her in the arm. They were humble people; they carried the girl to a hospital and merely asked that she be helped. But even at that, the word spread until it reached the President himself. So that one fine day an enormous black automobile pulled up in front of the little girl's house, and she and her parents promptly got out of the back seat, smiling and loaded down with packages. The girl's arm was bandaged, but she looked just fine.

Immediately the whole neighborhood converged on the home where the auto was parked. The house was filled to overflowing with friends from the neighborhood and the relatives who had waited for the family's arrival. The girl's mother didn't leave out a single detail in describing the staff's attentions at the luxurious clinic, in explaining the scholarship that the President had awarded her daughter, and in displaying all the gifts. Meanwhile, her husband was telling these astonished visitors about his new job, which was also a part of the compensation for the child's accident. And the presence of the uniformed chauffeur—who smiled as he drank a soda—seemed to make what the bedazzled parents described even more magnificent.

When the automobile left later on, the neighbors departed from the modest house in silence; the grownups among them appeared deep in thought. And even though no one said a word, that same night many of the children were obliged to look at the stars in the open air, while underneath their breaths, their parents prayed that they might receive the "blessing" of the President. Then there was a brief suspension in the routine firings: the presidential advisors needed time to persuade their leader to use the people's anticipation of help to political advantage.

Over the months other incidents occurred, some of which were fatal. There were even one or two that were intentionally fraudulent—certain parents purposely wounded their own children—but this stratagem was countered when the President began using bullets specially marked in order to prevent false claims.

Later, when a vagrant was wounded, the category of "Adults" was created, which also necessitated creating an office for investigating the claims of those who somehow felt unfairly treated. Not long afterward, for example, a group of neighbors came forward to denounce certain opportunists who rented their backyards to people living further out and making them pay by the minute for their stay. Aware of the complaint and knowing that sooner or later they would be kicked out, those temporary tenants demanded in turn the use of a revolver with a better range than the one the President was in the habit of using. But to date no word has been released in this regard, although it has been decreed that the children of well-to-do families who are wounded (they compete with each other to expose themselves to the bullets) will not receive any compensation. At the same time, the sale of certain talismans that supposedly attract bullets was prohibited.

Humanitarian organizations had no choice but to make their displeasure known. But, although their reasons are completely worthy of consideration, it is ridiculous to think of suppressing the presidential custom. The people have become so used to it, find so much hope and satisfaction in its existence (the cities outside the capital are now demanding something similar), that it has become a virtual reason of state; perhaps the most important one. So much so, people say, that although apparently moved by the image of wounded people (detractors correct this, saying *his* image communicated to foreign countries is the real concern), the president had once more intended to halt the shootings, but an explicit threat from the Army stopped him. Others say that the President no longer does the shooting, and that some official takes his place; and they add that the President takes advantage of these moments to mingle with the people and share the risks. Those who deny this rumor, talk instead about officials disguised as the president, and about the electoral benefits in future elections. But these are all suppositions. Until now, no one has seen the President or any double in the streets. Indeed, the public even talks openly about their preference for a safe president who shoots off bullets from his garden into the night. So the only thing that continues to be real, night after night, is the existence of a grassy path, traversed by a man who every so often raises his arm and, perhaps with a grimace, fires his gun.

Translated by Joanne M. Yates

❧ *The Buddha's Eyes*

The morning was warm; the whole plaza seemed to be carpeted with the lilac-colored flowers of the jacarandas. I decided to sit down on one of the benches. After a while, I turned to a book that I had just bought. Engrossed in what I was reading, I scarcely noticed that someone had taken a seat at the opposite end of the bench. I paid no attention. Then, suddenly, a voice startled me.

"And what do you do, *señor?*" It was the man now seated next to me who asked the question.

Annoyed by the interruption and the question, I replied without raising my head:

"At this particular moment, I'm reading."

"What is it that you're reading?" he asked calmly.

"Something by Stevenson."

"Ah yes, fantasy," he observed disdainfully.

I turned toward him, now ready to respond sharply. I discovered then that I was talking with a blind man. Between his legs rested a white cane and his eyes were concealed by large dark glasses. He looked to be around seventy years old. He was neatly dressed and his general appearance suggested a meticulous concern for grooming.

I reined in my annoyance and asked him in a friendly tone:

"Why the distaste for fantasy?"

He smiled briefly and then replied:

"No, not distaste. Just disagreement. Those literary tales get people into the habit of thinking about fantasy in terms of fiction. They appropriate the realm of the marvelous and turn it into a mere literary convention, leaving for life itself, like so many crumbs, what we consider as reality. And of course when the fantastic occurs in our reality, it is received with an irritated shrug, if not open hostility, as if it were a sort of inappropriate and annoying intrusion. To put it into simple words: literature discredits the fantastic."

He uttered all this in an uninterrupted flow, as if he were reciting it. When he finished, he removed his glasses and looked in my direction. I was shocked; those eyes were alive, not the eyes of a blind man. He seemed to sense my surprise, because he explained:

"Don't be alarmed. I'm not deceiving you. I am truly blind. People who see my eyes are always taken aback and doubt that I am sightless. And in a certain sense they are right, except that they cannot begin to imagine what the explanation is. As for now, if you care to interrupt your Stevenson for a while, I will tell you the story of my blindness, which has nothing whatever to do with fiction, although the whole matter is completely fantastic."

He stopped, awaiting my reply. The book that remained opened in my hands fell shut by itself. The man took note of this and apparently accepted it as my response to his question, because he began his story.

"My name is of no importance. I am now retired, but when my story began I was a sixth-grade teacher. All my life was devoted to teaching and you know what that means in this country. But I have no complaint. Well, then. I live in an apartment on Paraguay Street. Near my home there is an antique shop. Whenever I passed by it, I would stop for a while in front of the store window to look over the bronze and marble statues that were the specialty of that shop. One morning I noticed that next to a large marble Mercury there had been placed a small figure of Buddha. I was never very interested in oriental objects, but that miniature statue attracted me in strange way. Perhaps it was merely because of its disproportionate size alongside the other pieces. It seemed to have been placed there by mistake. Or maybe it was because, without being an expert on the subject, I saw that this was not one of those awful plaster statues that you see everywhere, but rather an instance where the carving and the painting of the details were those of a true artist. Furthermore, the curious attraction that it held for me could also have been explained by the fact that the eyes had not been painted on. That's right, the area where the eyes would be was left the almost white color of the wood, as if the creator of the statue had died suddenly, leaving his work unfinished. The consequence of that omission was a startling, almost grotesque effect. For some time I regarded the little eyeless god. In the days following I stopped several times to look at it. I even gave some thought to buying it. But considering my modest resources, I was forced to abandon the idea.

"One afternoon I was there looking at the statue. At that moment a man came out of the shop and asked me if I was interested in anything in particular. I pointed to the Buddha. He smiled and invited me to step inside. He went to the window and took out the sculpture; it was made of wood and was very heavy. Now that I had it in my hands I could see that I was not mistaken in attributing it to a first-rate artist. The perfection of the carving and the exquisite precision of the paint strokes were extraordinary, especially in the features of the face and in the folds of the robe, whose bluish color was an ideal background for the cranes that were depicted there, flying above a sleeping dragon. The sockets for the eyes had been carved out but, as I mentioned, they had not been painted in.

"'Place your index finger on the Buddha's navel and make a wish,' the shop owner said with a smile.

"*I hope it's not too expensive,* I thought ironically as I did what he suggested.

"Responding as if I had spoken out loud, the man pointed out:

"'Don't concern yourself with the price. And don't be surprised. This isn't the first time I've seen you outside, admiring the statue. It's really unusual, isn't it, despite the matter of the eyes? I'm offering a low price precisely because of its condition. Neither of us can have any illusions about its worth. Besides, it isn't even an antique. Look here, to be honest with you, it turned up in a chest that we bought at an auction for one of our other shops. So, let's see. What would you say to picking it up for . . . '

"It was a figure much lower than the one I had imagined. I bought it without hesitation.

"Back at home, I began to examine the little statue closely. I looked for some sort of inscription or something that might reveal its origin. But I found nothing. I also thought of taking it to an art restorer to have the eyes painted on, but in the end I didn't do so. I set it on top of a sideboard next to the window and there it remained. Each afternoon I would sit down before it and enjoy just looking at it. At times when I picked it up and gazed at it for a long time, a sense of sad helplessness came over me because its empty eyes seemed to acquire an expression of innocent questioning, like that of a homeless child. Puzzled by this, I would then let it rest on my lap, as if it were some sort of small pet, and then, when it grew dark, I returned it to its place.

"Several days passed. One afternoon I was walking home from school. It was early spring and a stiff breeze was blowing. Then a few blocks farther on, it suddenly started to rain. Looking for shelter, I took refuge beneath the awning outside a shop. The downpour increased. As I backed up under the awning, a combination of colors, boxes and paintings drew my attention to the shop window and at the same instant a pair of tiny almond-shaped objects crossed before my line of vision. I pressed up against the window for a moment, and then, as if forced in by the rain, I entered the store and at the appearance of the first clerk, I ordered paint and brushes. The statue, finally, would have its eyes.

"When I left the shop, the rain had stopped and the dark clouds had begun to break up. Eager to get back home, I took a taxi.

"On the sideboard, a single ray of sunlight illuminated the Buddha. I prepared the paint carefully, practiced a bit with a piece of cardboard and then got ready to do the job.

"When I began, my hands were trembling. Fortunately, the places for the eyes were well shaped and all it took to accomplish the task was to make sure that the paint didn't spread beyond the margins. The eyelashes required more pains.

"I don't know how long it took me to finish the eye. When it was done, I stepped back to have a look. I was astonished; the eye that I had just painted was perfect. You could almost think that it was alive. Suddenly, I felt dizzy. But the sensation passed quickly. I sat down in an armchair to rest for a moment; from there I regarded the Buddha. Soon I began to sense that it was looking at me and the unpainted eye struck me as some sort of mocking wink. With an impatient tingling in my hands, I started painting the other eye.

"I laid down my brushes around midnight. As I applied the last stroke, I had to rub my eyes; some sort of haze was clouding my vision. Then I glanced anxiously at the statue; but I was immediately relieved to see that the second eye seemed as perfect as the first. If there actually was any difference between them, this could only add to the lifelike impression that they communicated together. In fact, for a few moments, until I reminded myself of what I was looking at, I had the impression that I was gazing into the eyes of a real person, since the pupils, which I had given much effort to, emitted a kind of intermittent twinkling, as if giving off a surprising display of forms and colors.

"Moved by what I had just achieved, I felt the need to sit down. I sat there for some time, my mind blank, just staring at the statue. Then I carried it over to its place. In the shadows, the lively glimmer of the eyes continued. After resting a long gaze on the Buddha, I went off to bed, exhausted.

"The next day the effect did not strike me as so surprising. The lacquer on the eyes had clouded over somewhat, so that the difference between them and the rest of the body did not appear significant. Nonetheless, I decided not to varnish over the eyes, so that the overall effect would be consistent. I considered that in this way in time the Buddha would appear to have been painted by the same hand."

The man paused and rubbed his eyes. A sad expression came over his face. I remained silent. He blinked his eyes several times, as if trying to make order out of an onslaught of different images, and continued the story.

"It is at this point," he said in a thin voice, "that the terrifying part begins. It happened this way: some twenty days after having finished the statue's eyes, and while I was in class drawing several geometrical designs on the chalkboard, I noticed that the greenish color before my eyes began to take on a uniform brownish hue. I rubbed my eyes for a few seconds. When I opened them I saw before me a kind of beige-colored wall; with three large stains on it. Along one side I saw a much larger greenish vertical stain. That was all. I turned toward the students; the surface that confronted me turned with me, so that even while I could hear their murmuring, I could not see them, because of that stained wall. Trying not to call attention to my movements, I felt my way to my desk and sat down. A student asked me if there was something wrong. I replied that I had a headache and told the class to copy the designs on the chalkboard. Slowly I began to move my gaze about the room; but what I saw was always the same.

"When the class ended and the students left, I stood up and tried to move toward the door. At that moment the image before my eyes was taking on a clearer outline and became more defined. I stopped then, feeling that I was close to fainting. What I was seeing was, as I had suspected, a section of a wall where pictures were hung, while the larger shadow was in reality a doorway. But—listen carefully to what I am saying—everything I saw corresponded to a part of my house! To a wall of the living room, to be exact. I could not possibly have been mistaken. In front of the wall with the paintings was the window and the armchair where I sat every evening—and next to it the sideboard with the Buddha on it . . . The Buddha! What I was seeing was exactly what was situated opposite it. I tried to stay calm. I had arrived at the door.

I went out into the hall and, feeling my way along the wall, I headed toward the main office. The custodian saw me and ran over to help. Confused, I couldn't understand what was happening. *I don't know. I can't see anything,* was all I could say to him.

"Then, in the office, surrounded by my colleagues, I continued repeating that I couldn't see anything. I wanted to keep them from thinking that I was suffering from delusions, or something worse. They suggested calling a doctor. I said no, that I just wanted to be taken home. The principal put me in his car and took me back to my house, using my phone to call a friend of his who was a physician. I had a hard time persuading him that I needed to be alone. Finally he left, promising to call me after a while.

"Now by myself, I went to the sideboard. Scarcely had I placed my hands on the statue when the image of the wall began to tremble. When I picked it up, everything around me began to spin. I placed it in front of the window; suddenly that was the image before my eyes. I could no longer have any doubt about what was happening: the Buddha was seeing with my eyes. Or rather, I was seeing with his. How that terrifying transference had occurred I had no way of explaining. But the fact remained that I was now blind. I no longer recall what went through my mind that evening. Doubtless surprise, fear, incomprehension. But also much more than that.

After a while I began to move through the house, holding the Buddha out in front of me. This offered no problems. I tried covering the statue's eyes; it was as if I were covering my own. I went into my bedroom, turning out the lights and shutting the door. At first all I saw were shadows, but little by little as the Buddha's eyes became accustomed to the darkness, my vision improved. Eventually, I was able to make out clearly the shapes of the furniture. I went back into the living room. For a moment I had the urge to rub those very eyes that I had painted. But I resisted doing so for fear of becoming totally blind. It was absurd, but I now was totally dependent on that statue and its eyes. At that moment the doorbell rang.

"After setting the Buddha in its place, I went to open the door. It was the doctor. I let him examine me without uttering a word about what had actually happened. After a lengthy exam, he asked me several questions. Just to test his findings, I said that I could see some light, but only in a vague way. In response, he merely cleared his throat. He finished by taking information on me and giving me an appointment for the following day. Perhaps with the clinic's diagnostic equipment he could determine what was wrong with me. After he left, I went over to the Buddha and turned it to face the street; darkness was falling. Confused, I felt like crying. I thought of going back to see the antique dealer to find out the history of the statue, of taking it to my appointment the next day and revealing the truth to the doctors. I was weighing these possibilities when the phone rang. I had to explain to the distraught principal that not until after my examination on the following day would I know what my problem was. At his insistence, I agreed to have him bring his car by the next morning.

"At the Eye Clinic, after a series of rigorous tests, I was diagnosed as being totally blind, the result of causes unknown. I recall certain comments by the physicians concerning how "dead" my eyes appeared to them. Hearing those remarks, I had to suppress a smile; before leaving home I had taken the precaution of wrapping a cloth around the statue.

"As one might expect, I was granted immediate retirement, and the school arranged for a loan with which I could buy the rented apartment I had been living in. So that in short succession, I became a pensioner, a property owner, and blind . . . The latter condition, of course, was relative. While I had the Buddha I could see. In fact, it was possible for me to see without being in its presence, since I found I could place the statue in one spot and then move away. I could also watch television, read, and do quite a number of other things. But leaving the apartment, on the other hand, was a problem, since everyone considered that I was completely blind. I had to buy this cane and these dark glasses. Then, since it was hard to pretend that I needed the cane to move about, I had to practice at home until I developed a certain ease at doing it. Nevertheless, I did not leave home without the statue. I just needed to carry it discretely. A few months later I was given another examination, which resulted in the same diagnosis. By then I had adapted completely to my new condition and transported the statue without arousing any suspicions."

He paused again. A smile of satisfaction came over his face, as if reflecting his pleasure at deceiving those about him. But then he quickly turned serious and then seemed pained. He sighed several times and resumed his narrative.

"Well," he said, grimacing, "we now come to the final series of events that will bring me, to use the words of Stevenson, 'to the heart of darkness.'"

"Words of Conrad," I said correcting him.

"Oh, well, of course . . . But anyway, one evening I went out, as was my custom, to the Confitería del Molino, which was very familiar to me because I had been going there for many years. In a small box, with its sides fitted with transparent panels, I carried the little statue. In this way my vision was perfectly clear. I was approaching the tearoom when I was suddenly blinded by a kind of red flash. I stopped, rubbed my eyes and stretched the cane forward. There was nothing there. Almost immediately I recovered my vision, but once again I experienced the sudden flash of color, although this time it was not so intense.

"Its central portion began spreading out to the sides until it encompassed the entire width of my vision. Now I was confronted by something resembling a mist of red smoke, whose consistency was variable, since for a brief moment it thickened and clouded my view and then almost immediately that mist was shot through with streaks of light. I tried to take a few steps, but I was disoriented. I moved the box to the left and right in vain. The smoke did not disappear. I moved forward a few feet, guiding myself by the sounds around me. I came up against a wall and felt a hand touching one of my arms.

"'Do you want to cross the street?' said a voice that seemed very distant.

"No, I'm trying to get to the Molino," I replied, as I struggled to penetrate the cloud that prevented me from seeing.

"'It's quite nearby. Come with me.'

"I sensed that the man who was guiding me was opening a door and I felt another hand taking me by the arm and leading me to a table, where I felt my way into a chair like some sort of sleepwalker. I was so focused on the red vision that I hardly heard the voice that was addressing me:

"'*Señor* . . . *Señor* . . . Good evening. The usual?'

"It was the waiter who regularly served me.

"Yes, yes," I said with annoyance. "The usual."

"Without a word he left.

"Alone, I placed the container in my lap and tried to identify some object in the mist that continued to swirl before me. Reacting involuntarily, I tried with my hand to brush aside that cloud, which was thickening again. I was about to move both hands in that effort when I heard the sound of the waiter placing my order on the table. I sat up stiffly and tried to act as if I had the image of the tearoom in front of me. But once more my head and body bent forward, because a form was beginning to emerge behind the cloud, the darker areas of which were beginning to thin out. Finally, I saw before me a small room that resembled an artist's studio and that was illuminated by candlelight. On the left and right, before hanging drapes decorated with oriental characters, several incense-burners were emitting the red smoke that had first clouded my view and that now rose up in slender columns, dispersed here and there by wafting currents of air. In the center of the room, next to a wooden bedstead covered with a scarlet cloth, was an old man with Asian features. His body, wrapped in a light blue kimono with yellow edging, was swaying rhythmically, as if matching the tempo of a languorous song. Then suddenly, as his outstretched hands framed the scene, two women, similarly clad in kimonos, emerged from the far darkness. They advanced, making reverent bows to the old man. One of them was leading the other, whose steps were hesitant. When they stopped at the old man's side, I could see that they were an elderly woman and a young girl. It was the latter who seemed reluctant. The other woman appeared to be a servant, to judge from the respect that she showed toward the girl, who stood with her head bowed and her hands enclosed in the kimono in an attitude of total submission. They stood motionless for a moment. Then, acknowledging a sign from the old man, who had now become still, the older woman began to undress her mistress.

"When her kimono and undergarments were shed, the girl involuntarily moved her hands to cover her nakedness. But the old woman whispered something in her ear and the girl dropped her arms to her side. Then she raised her head and her glance fell on me. She was blind! In her large, almond-shaped eyes the corneas appeared lifeless, the color of pale jade in whose center could be seen the fleeting, unfocused movement of the pupils of a slightly darker shade. At the sight of that blank stare, my eyelids closed instinctively for a moment; but that image, of course, did not disappear. It became even more terrifying because the girl's repeated blinking, as if she were trying to penetrate a curtain of shadows, ultimately gave to her face the awful appearance of some creature that had emerged from deep, viscous earth.

"Fortunately, as soon as her eyes half-closed that impression vanished, since her features, as well as the form of her body, were models of perfection, and they recovered the serene grace of an Oriental princess. With a sense of sadness I remembered my Bu. . . . Here I came to my senses. Distracted by the details of that vision, I hadn't realized that what I was witnessing must have been a hallucinatory dream or something similar, because I found myself at a table in a downtown cafe and on my legs was resting, quiet and intact, the Buddha. What did all these fantastic images mean? Where did they come from, what time did they belong to? . . . The rumbling sound of thunder outside and the murmur of the other customers in the cafe intruded in a mocking fashion into my thoughts and the persistent nature of that vision only seemed more grotesque. But its power was so strong that in a matter of seconds I found myself once more immersed into its reality.

"The young girl had now lain down on the bed, completely naked, and the older woman had moved to the back of the room and stood in front of a blue folding screen. The old man was kneeling in a prayer-like posture. From the incense burners, the reddish smoke rose steadily. After a moment, the old man stood up and moved in my direction. He stopped right in front of my face and before I could react everything began swirling around me. Then, without a warning, the vague form of the girl slipped to one side and immediately her face and then her lips, which pressed together as if for a kiss, occupied my field of vision. This lasted for only a few seconds. Then, as quickly as they had approached, the mouth, the face, the body of the girl drew back until she was once again stretched out at my feet on the scarlet-covered bed. As I was still overcoming that sense of dizziness, something off to one side caught my attention. I looked up and could not suppress a moan. For on the wall facing the girl's feet, the vantage point from which I had previously been looking, a mirror reflected the figure of the old man who was holding in his hands . . . a statue identical to the one I had. It was the same in every way and, of course, had the eyes painted in.

"I can't describe the astonishment I felt on seeing it. I tore awkwardly at the material of the box and my fingers rubbed over the Buddha's eyes. The vision, however, continued uninterrupted. It was apparent that I was seeing through the eyes of that other statue. But—and here I was unsure—could it really be another one . . . ? A loud burst of laughter in the tearoom helped me to recover my sense of awareness. I tried to take a drink, but my hands remained fixed on the statue. I think I even made an effort to get up and walk out of the place, which struck me as somehow being under a spell, but my legs weakened and a confused series of images compelled me to fall back in the chair.

"Apparently, the old man had placed the statue back in its original location, because now I was viewing the scene from the former perspective. The girl was still lying there. A certain tenseness was tightening her body, even though her attitude was one of total passivity. The old man now knelt next to the bed and dipped his fingers into a bronze bowl. He stood up and moved to the head of the bed. He joined his hands together over the girl's head and murmured a few words as he stared fixedly at the statue. Then he bent forward and placed his hands on the girl's breasts. She shuddered, opened her eyes and looked in the direction of the statue. She then half-closed her eyelids, grasped the sides of the bed and waited.

"At first, the old man's hands softly massaged her flesh, as if he couldn't overcome the turgid firmness of her small breasts. After a moment, he increased the pressure and soon the delicate flesh began to show between the fingers of those claw-like hands. The old man grimaced as if from some pain, and his hands persisted. The old woman remained where she was, closely watching the movements of the old man, whose hands were coursing over the girl's shoulders and arms more forcefully. When the pressure of the moist fingers decreased a little, the feminine flesh exuded a faint bluish vapor that gathered in wisps before the old man's face.

"Despite not being able to grasp what was happening to me, I still found that my attention was fixed on what was occurring in that room, a scene that I also could not comprehend. There were moments when I considered it an obscene massage that might have some healing power; and then others when I thought I was witnessing a kind of heretical liturgy, a furtive imitation of some sacred ritual. I scarcely heard what was going on around me. Not only that, but so powerful was the effect of that vision on my being that I began hearing the sounds that would have been heard in that room. I noticed too that at times my hands were mechanically repeating the old man's movements.

"He had drawn closer to the girl's waist and his trembling hands were now resting on the dark patch of hair that covered her sex. (For the first time the old man's face suggested an expression of ecstasy, and the girl had grown pale.) When he removed his hands from that place, the old man stood up and began to tremble. He recovered quickly, however, and his gaze turned to the Buddha. He seemed exhausted and was breathing through his mouth. But his task was not over.

"He moistened his fingers once again in the bowl and began rubbing the girl's legs. The girl's body gradually began to stiffen and her soft curves, like polished ivory, reflected the light of the candles with a growing radiance.

"When he finished rubbing her legs (he gave much time to her feet), the old man stood up and went to the table where the Buddha sat. He opened a drawer and returned to the girl's side carrying a small black box. He removed from it a gem that resembled a sapphire and placed it in the bowl. The liquid seemed to boil. He waited a moment and then dipped his hands in carefully. Once his fingers were sufficiently moistened, he went to stand at the girl's feet and without hesitation bent over her.

"I tried to repress a warning shout, because I thought he was going to harm her. But the old man merely resumed with the rubbing he had done before, now, however, with more urgency and force. Alarmed by the sudden increase in movements, the old woman moved forward a few feet and stepped back only when the old man gestured sharply to her. She nonetheless kept her gaze on the girl, whose face was beginning to reveal a grimace of pleasure, which only moments before, considering the delicacy of those features, I could never have believed possible.

"I was sickened and, even though I knew it was useless, I closed my eyes. The old man, twisting like a worm spinning silk, hovered over the girl's body and his fingers continued to draw out of the glossy flesh the bluish vapors of a voluptuousness of indescribable scope.

"Nothing would remain on that skin—I thought—for other fingers to explore, nor would any caress ever signify anything for her, since the fingers of that sorcerer were occupied in extracting every last trace of the breath of the most intimate sensations, the vapor that was condensing as a kind of tribute before the little Buddha.

"Sorrowfully, in the presence of a perfect image of the girl that seemed to be suspended in the air above the bed and that contained the froth of a drained femininity, I began to comprehend something about that strange scene. In readings that I had done I had learned something about propitiatory rituals and personal offerings. Still, I was unable to determine the purpose of that ceremony. For that reason I needed to remain attentive and be open to the meaning of what was happening in that room.

"For a time the rubbing continued, however, without the violence displayed before. From time to time, amidst gasps and contortions, the girl opened her eyes and sought out the Buddha. Almost without being aware of it, I found that it was I who was observing her with a mixture of pity and misgiving. When the contortions of the two finally subsided, the girl recovered her expression of impassivity and the old man let his arms and head hang down, alleviating the stiffness that his efforts had produced in him.

"The old woman, who had been watching wide-eyed from a distance, approached and spread a blanket over the girl. The old man then turned away from the bed, knelt down, lifted his eyes to the Buddha and began to move his lips. When he finished the prayer, he stood up and went to the statue. As he took it into his hand, my vision was disturbed. He went back to the table and knelt before the girl. With a gesture of irritation, she had thrown the blanket to the floor and was stretched out before me like an opaque ribbon of silver. Suddenly, the old man raised his arms and lowered the statue into the mist that floated motionlessly above her. Then, drawing with it the mist in a gliding movement, the angle of my vision was once again fixed at the level of the girl, whose body I could hardly see, immersed as it was in that darkish cloud. There was, however, a sudden vibration and immediately afterward, as a shadow sprinkled with glowing white lights emerged and diminished the mist with the energy of its movement, the face of the young girl appeared before me with the overwhelming clarity of a nightmare.

"A shudder ran through me and my eyes, in direct contact with the enormous brightness of hers, went dim for a moment. When my vision returned, the young girl's form stood out clearly once more beyond the mist and the blank white eyes blinked with the mesmerizing power of a beast lying in wait. I tried to escape from that gaze that seemed to seek out my eyes, but all I could do was twist my body helplessly. I tried to calm down. I took a deep breath and . . . But I had to hold my breath because the girl's eyes began to grow larger—or perhaps it was that the old man was moving the statue closer to her face. In any case, the two white almond shapes continued to grow steadily until the moment when they became so intolerably close that they merged and I found myself looking into a luminous void where small reddish clouds were moving about and from whose depth began to emerge the silhouette of the old man, who was making a rubbing movement with his hands on the Buddha's face. His image grew steadily until finally, huge and shapeless, it was cast into my eyes.

"I reacted by moving back instinctively, since I had the impression that I was toppling into that void that once more stretched out before me. But suddenly, as if it had somehow rebounded, the man's outline appeared again. It moved backward slowly until all of his body could be seen and then stopped.

The vision was now clearer, although at times it seemed vague and transparent. I looked at his hands: one of them was grasping the statue; the other one was moving rhythmically over the Buddha's face. A familiar worry caused me to shudder when I saw that and my fingers came to rest protectively on the statue's eyes.

"But a moment later, without my willing it and seemingly motivated by the attitude of the old man, on whose face a smile was beginning to form, my fingers began gently rubbing the Buddha's eyes. The image of the old man suddenly became almost transparent and his movements seemed to cease. Now my own will asserted itself and I increased the pressure. I wanted that image to disappear. But my effort succeeded only in causing its outline to waver a bit, the way a reflection in a pool is disturbed by a gentle breeze. I gave up the attempt and decided to stop my rubbing. I could not! My hand did not respond. It continued rubbing as if it were not part of my body. Not just that: the rhythm of its movement was the same as that of the old man, who in spite of my earlier impression, had not stopped rubbing the Buddha's face. I tried to separate the hand that was holding the Buddha; I could not do that either. And, trying to stand up, I found that my legs too were ignoring what I was willing them to do. In a word, I was paralyzed. Only my eyes were capable of some slight movement. For several minutes I remained in that troubled state, with my fingers servilely imitating the old man's actions.

"Finally, with a shudder, I reacted and the frustration that was gripping me gave vent to the most ludicrous attempt, an insane effort to overcome the barrier of space—and maybe time as well—that separated me from that image and obliterate it. It was true, I could not stand for one more second that hateful smile that reflected the complacency of someone who is seeing his will carried out.

"Since I could succeed in moving my hands only feebly, all the helpless fury that had accumulated inside me was directed to them. In them, the most powerful efforts that I could imagine were rendered useless, the liberating blows that I imagined I could strike at the old man's image, the will to reach out and crush that merely left my arms seized with cramps . . . I don't know if at that moment I was aware of a kind of transposition that was forcing me to collaborate with what I was trying to destroy. But even if this were so, neither the rubbing nor the rage were the products of my will, so I perceived no consequences; I simply continued compulsively and stubbornly rubbing the statue.

"After a moment, I began using my fingernails, and then, unexpectedly, dark gashes began to appear on the man's body, which then started to bleed as I dug my nails in deeper. Yet in spite of my efforts, it seemed impossible to make that hated figure disappear. I felt my fingernails splitting, but still it resisted. I paused for a few moments in an attempt to overcome my agitation. I hadn't even noticed that the ability to move my hands had returned. Increasingly more frantic and determined, I kept up the rubbing and scratching until at last my fingers, my eyes and even the beating of my heart were held in suspense in the presence of the shadow that began to be defined beyond the ashen-colored cloud. Then there occurred something like a rapid movement, a spasmodic agitation within the cloud and suddenly, as if in a dream, a woman's face emerged, triumphant, her dark eyes now alive with vision . . . It was not more than a brief second, yet the young girl's image was impressed on my pupils like a perfect engraving. At this moment darkness flooded over my soul and my upper body fell forward onto the table, while my heart, burdened with the weight of an unbearable tension, seemed to accompany that metamorphosis with the vibration of its uncontrolled beating . . .

"I lay there for a moment on the table, trembling all over. Then, as if to aggravate the sensation of complete exhaustion that I was experiencing, an unrecognized force took me by the shoulders and shook me violently. Finally it released me and I heard a voice that gradually became clearer as I came to my senses. The voice was demanding:

"'*Señor, señor.* Are you all right? We're going to close now.' It was the waiter, who was trying to assist me.

"One of my hands reached out for the glass of water. I took a long drink. The waiter remained at my side. Then I heard him place something on the table. It was then that I noticed that my other hand was empty. I moved my hand over the table and found the statue. I took it eagerly and my blistered fingers moved to its eyes: the paint was gone. For a moment I caressed the small unpainted ovals, then placed money on the table to cover the bill and let the waiter lead me to the door. Outside, the moist air caused by the recent rain cooled my burning cheeks. I headed toward my house like an automaton, holding the useless statue in one of my hands. Fortunately, the street was deserted and the way back was familiar to me.

"When I arrived home, I felt strangely serene. The questioning that at first had slowed my steps had disappeared. Can a fly possibly explain the web and what spins it . . . ? When I entered my apartment, I tossed the statue onto a chair. Then I went into my bedroom. In the state of exhaustion that I found myself in and, who knows, perhaps also feeling freed from the threat that had accompanied me ever since the day when I was forced to depend on the Buddha's eyes, I immediately fell asleep.

"In the days following, up until the moment when images of past events reappeared in my brain, the young girl's face, its final image was all that accompanied me. Believe me that that vision, which became increasingly alluring, had the effect of erasing from my mind any need of an explanation. In her presence, everything seemed to be justified, even my blindness. I even began to feel—and to some degree I still do today—that this entire experience had happened to someone else and that I was nothing but a passive observer, in whose presence the Fantastic had revealed once again the magnificence of its unceasing magic ... *The unceasing magnificence of the Fantastic.* Why not? Could there be any better ... justification for my adventure?

"As for the statue, a package with a false sender's name returned it to the antique dealer's shop. And even though I haven't gone by there again (nor do I plan to), I still have the sense that in the store window, blind and perhaps unnoticed, a little wooden Buddha is shuddering with the voluptuousness of a young woman that, like a coursing sap, runs through it s blessed, insatiable veins."

Translated by D.A.Y.

❧ *The Calendar*

Every day, around dusk, the man would quietly enter the neighborhood bar and, leaning on the counter, ask for a brandy. He was short in stature, rather thin, mild-mannered, and well along in years. His face, barely distinguished by the mustache of an outmoded style, spoke more of loneliness than of the years. He wore a wrinkled brown suit, but was otherwise neatly dressed. A weakened heart had forced him into early retirement and since that time he had lived alone in a room in a nearby boardinghouse.

The bar was inevitably crowded with boisterous regulars. Some played cards at their tables; others strolled about, glass in hand, engaging in the easy camaraderie stimulated by alcohol. The man knew almost all of them by sight, but did not exchange greetings with any of them. When the barman filled his glass, he habitually took a first sip and paused to look around the bar for a moment. He would then turn back and from then on his gaze would not stray from a small illustrated calendar that had been affixed with a thumbtack to one of the shelf supports behind the counter. It was one of the familiar playing card–sized calendars, of the kind that can be carried in a billfold, on which was displayed the image of a blonde woman (*gringa,* was the man's term for her) completely nude and kneeling on a large green pillow. Her figure (which grime and dust had obscured a bit) seemed to suggest a kind of innocent voluptuousness, a mixture of insinuation and helplessness. It must have been a long-outdated calendar, because when the man first began to frequent the bar, several years before, it was already there.

At the outset he had given it the same casual attention that he paid to the dusty bottles that lined the shelves behind the counter. But after a while, little by little, he became aware that his glance was resting for longer periods on the calendar card. Later on, he realized that he was formulating questions about the woman who appeared on it. Eventually, both alarmed and gratified, he discovered that he was unable to go a single day without seeing the old calendar card.

After that, he was an unfailing visitor. When darkness began to fall, he would leave the boardinghouse and hurry to the bar, where he remained with his dreamy gaze fixed on the picture, for some two or three hours. Then, when some garrulous drunk approached him, or when his legs began to weaken, he would offer a last toast to the girl on the calendar, pay for the drinks and return to his room.

One night, the man found himself at the bar looking at the calendar. A third drink was in his hand. At that moment the bar had only a few customers, but they were nonetheless typically noisy. Suddenly, a gust of frigid wind blew open the door. The man felt the chill with a shock and turned around.

At that moment the outline of a blonde woman passed by the open frame of the door, which fell shut again. It was a brief vision, almost fantasy-like, but it was sufficient to startle the man, who, once he had recovered from his surprise, anxiously turned his gaze back to the calendar, as if to confirm what he had seen. Then he dug into his pocket, threw a few wrinkled bills on the counter and went out. A gust of wind whipped across his face and brought on in him a fit of coughing. When he recovered, he began looking for the mysterious woman. But the street was deserted. He went around the corner and looked in all directions. There was no one in sight. He remained for a moment in front of the bar, trembling. Then he left in the direction of his boardinghouse.

He was numb and shaken when he arrived. It was hard for him to breathe. He loosened his shirt collar and then, with difficulty, climbed the first two or three stairs. Exhausted, he sat down on a step and leaned his head and shoulders against the wall. In a moment, he had fallen asleep.

Some time later he was startled when a man brushed past him on his way up the stairs. As if in a dream, he saw the fellow roomer look down and, attempting a gesture of sympathy, smile at him. He waited for a few seconds, then with great effort started up the stairway. He went directly to his room, which faced onto the second courtyard, and paused in front of his door. A faint, shimmering glow shone out through the transom. He did not remember having left a light on. Driven by something now more than curiosity, he entered his room.

Once inside, his apprehension was transformed into wonder, since on his bed, naked, smiling and displaying the same pose as on the card, was the girl on the calendar. Her body, which the man's gaze took in eagerly, gave off a crimson aura that was bright enough to illuminate the entire room, where everything was otherwise as he had left it: neat and orderly, down to the unread afternoon newspaper lying on the night table. Suddenly, the young woman began adopting different poses, holding each for a few moments. The man rubbed his eyes and for an instant had the sensation that someone was shuffling a deck of enormous erotic calendars. When the woman returned to the original pose and kept it, the man felt himself losing his balance and he almost fell. The young woman laughed at the man's confusion and gestured to him to come closer.

A dream, the liquor, he thought to himself as he moved forward. He stopped at the edge of the bed. The girl turned slowly and came to kneel before him. He saw now that she was younger than he had believed her to be. A delicate perfume emanated from her voluptuous body, whose physical charms were now presented to him in clearer detail within the enveloping glow. Her skin seemed to suggest an ineffable sweetness: *A magnolia moistened by the rain,* he thought, mistaking the tango lyric, as he shyly gazed at her full breasts, the small, firm waist, her open thighs and the golden fleece . . .

The unwavering smile on the woman's face gave him the courage to think of questioning her. But she was the first to speak. Moving her lips languorously, she uttered a few words in a language he did not know. Then, seeing that he did not respond, she motioned to him that he too should undress. The man reacted with embarrassment and retreated a few steps. But the girl's smile was so calm and provocative, and exuded such seductiveness and trust, that he felt his modesty being overcome, while at the same time the persistent sense of unreality was quickly fading. So that, within a moment or two, he was no longer regarding the girl as an apparition, but as a wife with whom one is reunited after a long separation. He removed his jacket and placed it on the back of a chair. When he turned back he saw himself reflected in the wardrobe mirror. Standing there, he took off the rest of his clothes. The glow coming from the girl's body seemed to draw him forward.

He stopped at her side at the edge of the bed. The girl drew away and lowered herself onto her back, assuming a pose of abandonment and surrender. A current of air brushed over the man's legs and, urged by the chill, he climbed onto the bed. An overwhelming warm scent brought him to the point of losing consciousness. But nonetheless he had the strength to approach and kneel before her, his gaze moving over her body. When his eyes reached her face, he stopped. The girl encouraged him with a gesture of her hand. Then the man moved forward. His ultimate joy was to sense, while his fallen body penetrated the luminous transparency, that something like the warmth of a kiss was going to soothe his encounter with the final darkness.

Translated by D.A.Y.

❧ Bárcena's Dog

"So, my Colonel, what do we do with the savage?"

One-Eyed Bárcena, officer in charge of a division of Oribe's forces that was bivouacked at that moment in San Nicolás de los Arroyòs, felt a twinge of anger and with his one good eye sought out the insolent fellow who had broken the silence. But as he looked up and down the orderly line of red uniforms, he realized that in truth it had been less the result of impudence than the desire on the part of the entire camp to know once and for all what their leader's decision would be. He suspended his search and turned again to the man, guarded by two soldiers with lances, who stood a few paces away before his tent. Once more he scrutinized the blue eyes, the long graying hair that was plastered to his sweaty brow, the beard trimmed in the shape of a "U," which labeled him as a Unitarian, the clothing of a man of breeding, and thought to himself that if it were merely a matter of punishing him for the poisoned bread that he had delivered to the camp that morning, just a few jabs with the tips of those lances would do, producing a slow loss of blood, or perhaps the best solution might be simply having his throat cut.

But there was something other than just the question of the bread, something so serious that no one in the camp was unaware of it. Several months earlier, this man (whose name was Suárez, a doctor by profession) had refused to interrupt the pregnancy of a girl who, on leaving La Rioja to be with Oribe's forces, had been received by him—Bárcena—as a gift from General Quiroga himself. And even though the matter had finally been settled, the act, the affront, now required a special form of torture. This was what was disturbing the troops, for Bárcena had not yet settled on just what that punishment would be.

The prisoner Suárez looked about absently at the woods surrounding the camp. That morning, when the party of soldiers sent by Bárcena broke into his house and accused him of poisoning the bread that as a well-off local resident he was obliged to send every day to the federal army, he had said goodbye to his servants (he had no family) with words of reassurance. It would be a simple matter to clear up the misunderstanding. But later at the camp, when he faced those who accused him of the poisoning, he understood that although the charge was completely false, Bárcena was not going to let him go. From that moment on, he no longer attempted to defend himself and would not speak. Unshaken, in spite of the jeering and the threats, he remained impassive, even when Bárcena, as he was doing now, stood before him and dug into his very soul with that ferocious eye.

Long live the Federals.
Their time has come.
Down with Unitarians,
Nothing but scum,

chanted a woman's voice at that point and the troops enthusiastically responded with a chorus of approval. Off to one side, a tied-up dog began barking.

Bárcena stepped away from Suárez to accept a *mate* that one of his aides had brought to him and signaled for someone to silence the dog. A soldier misunderstood the gesture and instead of quieting him, set him loose. The animal ran directly at Suárez and clamped his jaws on the calf of one of his legs. Suárez, who had his hands tied behind him, cried out and in the attempt to free his leg lost his balance and fell to the ground. The dog did not release his hold, even though his breathing was restricted by the fabric of the trousers. Leaping forward, Bárcena's aide grabbed the rope tied to the dog's neck and yanked it back. But he had to lay on the dog with his horsewhip before the animal would let go. For his part, Bárcena did not intervene in the incident. When they took the dog away, he continued sipping his *mate* and eyeing Suárez, whose leg, on examination, was judged not to be seriously injured. When he finished the *mate*, he gazed thoughtfully at the ground and then took a dagger from one of the soldiers, approached Suárez, now standing, from behind and with one slash severed the rope that immobilized his arms.

"This way you're equal," he said scornfully and went over to where the dog was still barking, in spite of the efforts of the soldier who was holding onto his collar.

"Put him on a leash," he said to the soldier. "And you. Defend yourself," he ordered Suárez bluntly.

Suárez looked at him incredulously, but seeing that the dog was approaching him again, he planted one leg and kicked out menacingly with the other. The dog became more enraged.

"Not that way, my friend. Do it like a dog," Bárcena interjected, in an almost fatherly voice.

Suárez stared at him as if he didn't understand what he was asking.

"The way a dog would. You bark and bite, too. Go on!" insisted Bárcena, who was now warming up to the idea.

"Come on, down on the ground! Didn't you hear the colonel?" said an officer, poking Suárez's shoulder with the tip of his lance.

"Right, down on the ground like a dog," urged the surrounding soldiers, closing in on them.

Suárez set his knees on the ground first and then, prodded by the tips of several lances, had to place his hands down as well.

A noisy circle of red appeared to swarm over him and the crazed dog.

"Bark! Bite him! Attack! Come on, savage," they heard Bárcena cry out.

"Yes, go ahead. Bark! Bite him!" the others immediately shouted in chorus.

Suárez looked at the dog's foaming muzzle and an expression of horror twisted his features. He closed his eyes, clenched his fists tightly and his body began to tremble. He recovered quickly, however, and when he looked again at the dog Suárez's expression had turned to one of determination. The cries of Bárcena and the soldiers together with the dog's barking now seemed to be reaching him from a distance. Suddenly, he drew his head down into his shoulders, and then when he raised it again a kind of whimper came from his mouth that seemed to surprise the dog and compelled the men to silence. He moved forward very slightly and repeated the sound. The observers gave out a howl that caused the dog to turn around in fright. Suárez, his back streaked with blood, crawled ahead a bit farther and with a grimace uttered twice a single syllable that for its hoarse resonance could have been a bark. The soldiers screamed their enthusiastic response and the dog, now totally terrified, shrank down close to the ground, whined and then desperately made for an open gap in the circle of men. The man holding the rope tied to the dog looked at Bárcena who, with a gesture, indicated to him to drop it. The dog, falling over his own legs, stumbled away amid the laughter of all.

"Savage!" they exclaimed as the dog ran off and then they turned toward Suárez who was looking in the direction the dog had taken. The lances had ceased to prod at his back, but the tears in his shirt revealed that he was still losing blood. Bárcena circled him thoughtfully.

"It seems to me that a dog like this one is exactly what we need here," he said to the corporal, as if just speaking to himself, but also expecting at the same time some reaction from the troops.

A mumbled agreement was the response he received.

"Of course," he hastened to add, "something has to be done to improve his bark. But we can work on that."

Standing before Suárez, he said:

"It's settled then, doctor. You are going to be my dog. The other one is worthless. Although, you understand," he added, moving closer to Suárez's head to speak, "you have another choice, if you want it. Be my dog or—"

"The *painkiller*," said one of the soldiers when Bárcena looked in his direction.

"The *painkiller*, yes. Very good. But the one with the dull blade, since we don't want people dying on us too quickly," said One-Eye, acknowledging the soldier's suggestion. He turned to an officer.

"All right then, captain. Lock this man up with a couple of dogs, so he can learn how to bark. And train him properly. The only people here who go around on two feet are federals."

A mixed reaction of amusement and surprise was the response to this statement of Bárcena, who promptly headed off with a few of his men toward his tent.

"Oh, yes," he said, turning back at the tent's entrance, "so that no one will mistake him for another dog, he'll have his own name, too. We'll call him 'Scum,'" he exclaimed as his gaze crossed that of a woman who was grinding corn and humming softly.

"Scum," the soldiers repeated as they watched Suárez being placed into a makeshift cage together with several dogs.

"Scum!" And with the uttering of that word, the first piece of raw meat was tossed into the cage.

II

Burdened with the details of Oribe's campaign, Bárcena limited himself in the following days merely to inquiring if his orders concerning Scum had been carried out. But one morning while he was drinking *mate* with his aides, a distant barking aroused his interest in having a look at him.

"Have Scum brought here to me," he ordered. "Let's see if he has learned anything."

They heard several dogs bark a few moments later and then, moving painfully on his hands and feet, Suárez entered Bárcena's tent. His clothes were in tatters and his arms were marked with scratches and bites. He was unable to stand up because in order to make him walk like a dog they had tied his bare feet to a stick that ran the entire length of his back. His filthy, matted hair together with his face and beard spattered with mud created the image of a primitive animal. With a critical eye, Bárcena took it all in. Then he asked:

"And how are we coming with the barking?"

The soldier who had brought Suárez in had no answer.

"Well, let's see then," said Bárcena, standing up in front of Suárez and smiling at his aides. "All right, Scum. Bark for me a little."

Suárez moved into another position, and lowered his head while his joints creaked. Then he sat motionless.

Bárcena sucked on his mustache and glanced at his men. He insisted once more:

"Let's have—"

"Hear me, my colonel. I—" Suárez interrupted in a choked voice, fixing his bulging eyes on him. Bárcena cut him off sharply:

"Shut up! You can't speak! You're a dog now and dogs bark. Do you hear what I say? They bark! So go ahead, bark! Bark!"

An expression of surprised incredulity appeared on Suárez's features, as if some sacred compact had just been broken. He then hung his head down and his body began to tremble.

Bárcena continued to wait, now angered. An officer who had been standing in a corner of the tent muttered something about an urgent necessity and left. The other men made joking allusions to a weak stomach and looked to see if Bárcena was joining in on their taunting. But he paid no attention to them. He was staring with a cold eye at Suárez, who seemed frozen in indecision.

"Scum . . . Scum," Bárcena called out, bending over Suárez, hands on his knees.

"Scum, Sc—"

A movement from Suárez interrupted him. Suárez had raised his head and was staring at him, a bitter hatred burning in his contracted pupils.

Caught off guard by the intensity of that gaze, Bárcena stood motionless for a moment. Then his hand moved slowly toward the dagger that he carried in his belt. But now the doctor's expression changed. As if he were trying to focus his vision, his eyes grew larger and acquired a look of near total resignation—that of a person who has sought another solution but finally has resigned himself to an unthinkable alternative.

"All right then, Scum. Good," Bárcena said encouragingly, in a calmer voice. Reaching down to stroke his back, he asked him once again to bark.

Suárez shook his head, his features slackened as if he were about to laugh, and from the midst of the muddied beard there came an unrecognizable sound, a sound that could not conceivably emerge from a human throat.

"That's right. That's right," said Bárcena, urging him on again.

Suárez scraped at the ground with his fingers and repeated the noise.

"Good. Very—"

A shot rang out in the middle of the campground and a bullet whistled over the top of the tent. Bárcena exchanged a quick glance with his men and then ran outside.

But it turned out to be nothing but an accidental firing. The officer who had left the tent a few moments earlier had unintentionally discharged his gun.

"Be a little more careful with your weapon, Leiva," scolded Bárcena and then turned to go back with his men to the tent.

Inside, Suárez had lain down on his side to relieve the pressure on his legs and was shaking his head in an effort to chase away the flies. Bárcena regarded him pensively and then observed:

"That's not bad for a beginning. But if I want to have a really good dog, I'm going to have to give a little more attention to the job."

And he motioned to the soldier to take Suárez away.

"I'll go with them," said one of the officers and he went out.

When they passed by Leiva, who was still examining his gun, the officer lagged behind a little and winked his eye.

"You ought to be more careful about aiming so low."

Leiva returned the wink and turned back to his gun.

III

For Bárcena, giving a little more attention to the job meant first of all transferring Suárez and the dogs to a larger cage made of bamboo and then placing him under the surveillance of a mulatto who was known as an experienced handler of horses and dogs. Bárcena allotted him three months to complete the job. Suárez was obliged to share the food (leftovers that the soldiers tossed in) with his cage mates and had to take care to follow all the orders given by the mulatto, who at the first sign of disobedience, stepped into the cage and distributed lashes with his whip. Every day Suárez was taken out to run (to crawl hurriedly) around the camp so that his joints could become accustomed to a more rapid pace. The trainer explained to him that Bárcena wanted a dog that would follow him when he rode his horse at a trot.

At times, when the mulatto got drunk, Suárez's suffering was intensified. For example, in view of the troops who could confirm his handler's achievements, he was forced into wagging his posterior to indicate his happiness as well as licking the mulatto's hands when they were held out to him at the end of the performance. If he failed to perform satisfactorily or displayed any kind of resistance, the whip lashes rained on his shoulders. Every two weeks he was paraded before a representative of Bárcena for the purpose of demonstrating his progress.

The men who made up the troop now no longer laughed so easily when they saw him crawling behind the mulatto. In fact they experienced a certain discomfort on seeing how far the matter had been pursued. Moreover, they attributed Suárez's docility to some kind of scheming on his part, and when the *mate* circulated among them or at mealtimes they entertained themselves predicting how the situation might end or imagining what possible type of revenge the doctor might succeed in carrying out. Leiva, the officer who had pretended to fire his gun accidentally in order to interrupt Súarez's torture, became less cautious and when the mulatto was not watching would throw eggs and peeled fruit into the cage. At times, too, he asked Suárez to be patient, since sooner or later the colonel was going to tire of the whole business and would release him. Suárez settled back into his corner of the cage and did not reply.

At the end of the third month of training, he was taken to Bárcena. He now wore only a kind of burlap loincloth that was wrapped over the remains of the trousers he was wearing on the day of his capture, and the pole had been removed from his back. His hands and feet were callused and his nails had grown out and now curved inward like claws. His face was not visible since his head, covered with matted hair, was always facing down. His movements were more fluid, although he could not prevent his knees from occasionally scraping the ground.

"Yes, I see we're making headway. But we're not there yet. There's still a way to go," said Bárcena at the conclusion of the show that, without the trainer's whip being spared, Suárez put on for him. Then he gave the mulatto two more months.

Suárez showed no outward emotion over the extended deadline, but as time wore on he began to display more resistance. He would not bark when asked to by the mulatto, he became more aggressive with the dogs and reacted with bites and swipes of his hands at the slightest attempt at punishment. He even seemed to be establishing a kind of rivalry between the two of them to see who would weaken first—the one who was delivering the blows or the one receiving them. Hearing about this change in demeanor, Bárcena would occasionally approach the cage to observe Suárez, who from his corner glared at him in a way that he did not know how to interpret.

The end to the second training period soon arrived. Bárcena was more satisfied this time and he relieved the mulatto of his duty. Suárez was tied to a tree so that he could guard the entire encampment.

"I don't want the least sound to be heard without you barking. Because around here, you never know," Bárcena ordered as a soldier secured the leash.

Suárez shook his mass of wild hair.

"And no one is to interfere with Scum," Bárcena declared to those who were present. "I'm the only one in charge now."

The men murmured assent and Suárez barked, twice.

IV

"So how does he fall short of being a dog, colonel? If you're thinking hair, you've got a regular wolf here."

Bárcena barely smiled at Colonel Santa Coloma's suggestion and kept his gaze on Suárez, who was lying at the foot of the tree, oblivious to the conversation of the two officers. The colonel had come to take leave of Bárcena before joining the advance forces of Oribe, who was preparing to cross over to Uruguay. Bárcena had taken that occasion to show him his mascot.

"Well, I don't know. Something's still missing," the one-eyed officer said, rising to accompany his colleague as he prepared to leave.

"Maybe a bitch at some point?" suggested Santa Coloma with a grin as he walked past Suárez, who was now watching them closely.

"Well, who knows. Just maybe . . ." replied Bárcena, and their parting was marked with laughter.

Nearly six months had passed since Suárez's removal from the cage. His appearance was terrifying: dirt and filth had darkened his body and over the calluses crawled large blue flies that he ignored. His snarled hair and the mud-stiffened beard formed a bizarre kind of helmet that barely left uncovered the area of his eyes on which the gray eyebrows cast an ashen shadow. The first two of those months had been particularly painful for him, since he was more accessible to Bárcena, who hardly let a day go by without requiring some demonstration of a dog's behavior. But later on, owing to his concern over the news of an imminent invasion, Bárcena gradually took less notice of him. Only when he received the visit of some important person did he return to his old habits and demand that Suárez bark at the visitor or have him savagely attack some soldier chosen for the occasion. In the meantime, Suárez became accustomed to spending each day stretched out on the ground and observing all the activities of the camp.

In time the soldiers stopped talking about him and even made an effort not to look his way, as if they distrusted that expression of apparent meekness provoked by even their slightest gestures. As for Leiva, he no longer brought him food. And when he felt Suárez's eyes on him, his body became tense and he lost no time in disappearing off among the tents. Suárez also grew uneasy at the sight of Leiva, especially at night when he would see him meet with two other men and, constantly glancing about him, speak to them in a low voice.

CASS DISTRICT LIBRARY
319 MICHIGAN RD 62N
CASSOPOLIS MI 49031

In the end, it was only Bárcena who did not avoid his gaze. Every morning, from the doorway of his tent, his glance would settle for several minutes on Suárez's face, as if he were fascinated by the spark of patient determination that those moments seemed to ignite on the doctor's countenance. "Scum!" he would then shout at him and step back into his tent, amused by the rapid lifting of Suárez's head on hearing the unexpected utterance.

V

One more month had passed, similar to those preceding it, when a horseman arrived with the news that the invasion of Uruguay had begun. The camp immediately acquired a mood of high-spirited excitement and Bárcena shortly afterward announced that in a few days they would move on to Entre Ríos.

"Well, now, Scum," he said to Suárez some time later, "we'll soon see how you behave in action," and he set out on horseback to join a group of other riders who were galloping around the camp shouting orders.

Suárez dragged himself along behind in an attempt to follow, until the rope restrained him. He clawed at the ground and a desperate look appeared in his eyes. Then he moved as far away from the tree as possible and when night fell he lay with his gaze fixed on Bárcena's tent, where the light remained lit until late. At dawn he fell asleep.

The camp awakened late that day. The troops, the officers and Bárcena himself, however, gave the appearance of having gotten little rest. Suárez remained at the far end of the rope and did not touch the food that they brought him at noon. Everything became calm again during the siesta and the evening turned imperceptibly into night. Suárez dozed for a while until he was suddenly awakened by a noise. Next to the tree a cart had been left with a cage on it, the means by which he would be traveling the next day. He looked toward Bárcena's tent. The light was on and to judge from the shadow cast from the inside, the colonel was organizing some papers. Still facing the tent, he settled down and a few minutes later went back to sleep.

He was awakened by the unusual brilliance of the moon and the sound of footsteps. Alert, he sat up, recognizing the silhouette of three men outlined against the background of tents. It was Leiva and the two men who often accompanied him. As they passed the tree, one of the men headed in his direction. The others continued toward the tent where Bárcena had not yet retired. Suárez grunted and pulled at the rope, but stopped suddenly. Leiva's companion had arrived at his side and held a knife in his hand.

"Easy, my friend. We've come to invite you to a party," the man said when he saw Suárez bare his teeth. With a single motion he sliced through the rope.

Suárez trembled and continued grunting. The man regarded him for a moment and then with another stroke cut through the thong that held his feet together. Ignoring Suárez's threatening demeanor, he took him by the arm and dragged him in the direction of Bárcena's tent, inside which a confused struggle of shadows was being played out. When they arrived at the door, he pushed Suárez in and remained outside.

Suárez fell heavily to the ground and emitted a startled grunt on seeing that Bárcena, a rag stuffed in his mouth, was being held from behind by Leiva's other companion. Leiva, displaying not the slightest haste, was preparing to slit Bárcena's throat. Bárcena's one eye opened wide in desperation, while his feet kicked at the overturned cot. Suárez stopped growling, his deformed hands stretched out, and he repeated the barely understandable syllable "No." His gaze met Bárcena's and as a fleeting series of expressions flickered in his eyes, the laboriously uttered "No" gave way once more to growling.

"So here we go. And the first cut is for Scum," said Leiva savagely as he prepared to administer the initial stroke of the knife.

But Suárez was too quick. With one leap he reached Leiva and sank his teeth into his throat. Leiva fell back, blood erupting from the wound, his arms pinned to the ground by the doctor's claws. The man who was holding Bárcena loosened his grip, but One-Eye did nothing to free himself. He stared in complete astonishment at how Suárez was gnawing at the neck of the man, whose feet were now flailing at the ground. When Leiva stopped moving, his companion moved away from Bárcena and fled out through the door. Bárcena removed the rag from his mouth and stepped back a few paces. On the floor, light was reflected off of the blade of Leiva's knife. One-Eye calculated the distance but did not move. Suárez had now released Leiva and looked up at him.

"Scum," Bárcena muttered in a thin voice, his wide-open eye staring at the mask of hair and blood before him.

Suárez crawled toward him, very slowly, and covered the knife with his foot.

"Scum," Bárcena repeated, extending his hand as if to protect himself.

But Suárez made one more move toward him, reached his head forward and, amid satisfied grunts, began to lick his hand.

Taken by surprise, Bárcena at first remained motionless. Then his eye glistened and as he bent over Suárez to stroke his back, he began repeating:

"Scum . . . Now you're being good. Now you're a good dog."

The doctor grunted contentedly and rubbed himself against him.

"Now you're good, Scum," Bárcena said for the last time as he stood up and turned to right the overturned cot.

At that moment, Suárez seized Leiva's knife and sat up. Bárcena noticed the movement and quickly turned back. In the instant before he collapsed to the floor, he was able only to utter an expression of surprise. Suárez leaned over the fallen body and, placing a hand on it, came close to observe the face of the dying man.

When Bárcena's eye finally closed, Suárez threw the bloody knife alongside Leiva, crawled outside and, with the entire camp asleep before him, he barked, and barked . . .

Author's Note: The incidents described in this story are true. They occurred in 1842 and are related in historical form by Julio Llinás and Manuel Cervera, and in the context of a fictional chronicle by the Spanish writer Ciro Bayo. Manuel Cervera's testimony is as follows:

" . . . We are going to describe here an occurrence that has been set forth elsewhere, and that we have heard related by the same veteran soldiers we have referred to before. While Oribe's army was quartered in San Nicolás, one day tainted bread had been delivered to the camp. By way of women's gossip, it was suspected that Dr. Durán had poisoned the bread and sent it to the camp. Colonel Bárcena had Durán arrested and, even though later it was learned that the claim against him was false, he remained under arrest, carrying out the role of a dog, tied up and locked in a cage into which chunks of raw meat were tossed. Bárcena, who had a personal grudge against Durán, became the dog's master. But Bárcena's aide, a man called Leiva, took advantage of Bárcena's absences to have soldiers release Suárez from his torment and saw to it that he was fed steak, eggs, etc. When Oribe moved on Entre Ríos and arrived at Las Conchas, establishing there his base for the invasion of Uruguay, an epidemic broke out that carried off 20 to 50 men each day. Durán said that he would treat those who had fallen ill and Oribe requested of Echagüe, who was the governor of Santa Fe, that Durán be allowed to do so. But Bárcena refused to hand him over. As a result of repeated demands, Durán was released and sent to Las Conchas where he did cure the troops and thereafter remained free under Oribe's protection. Overrulings of this sort of the will of a subordinate officer by his superior were common. Bárcena died in Salta, killed in a fight by Major Carlos Niera, leaving behind him a stained reputation."

From *History of the City and Province of Santa Fe* (1907), Vol. II

Translated by D.A.Y.

❧ *The Poem*

"You have exhausted the years and they have exhausted you,
And you still have not written the poem."
—Borges, "Matthew, XXV, 30."

When the author of *Gizeh* (the "Maestro," as everyone called him) received his fifth or sixth doctorate from one of the most important universities abroad, I, a mere admirer of his work, determined to meet him personally. I knew it wasn't hard to arrange an interview and in some cases all it took was a phone call. My first attempt, however, failed. A woman's voice informed me that for the time being the writer had suspended all new commitments. If I cared to, I could phone him later on.

I waited for about a month and called once more. The same voice answered. Now the writer was indisposed owing to some illness or other and, naturally, was seeing no one. I took an intense dislike to that woman, and my displeasure was further provoked by the thought that she might have lied to me. Besides, once again, our meeting was postponed, an encounter that, without my knowing why, was becoming increasingly important to me.

Without any hope that a third call might change my luck, I thought about some other way of approaching the Maestro. It seemed to me that in my capacity as an admirer I might well send him a gift together with a few lines wishing him good health. Despite its obviousness, the idea of a book occurred to me.

Knowing his preferences for Anglo-Saxon writers, I looked about in several bookshops for something interesting. But what was available seemed common and trite. Nearly resigned to giving up the search, something that I ingenuously associated with fate came to my aid. As was my habit, late one afternoon I visited a used bookshop on Calle Moreno. There, on a sale table, a goodly number of old books had been laid out, most of which were in sad condition. Looking through them, I noted that the majority were in French. Suddenly, my attention was drawn to a book bound in blue covers, with the front cover and spine singed. When I took it up, my fingers were blackened at the touch. Inside, some of the pages were darkened also. It turned out to be an edition of Marlowe's *The Tragical History of Dr. Faustus,* in English, with no indication of date or publisher, though it was clearly very old. Almost without thinking, I stepped to the counter. I had found the gift for the Maestro.

I dropped it off with the *portero* at his apartment building, enclosing a personal card with a few words of apology for the condition of the book.

Two or three days later, when I was beginning to doubt the advisability of my plan, I received a phone call from the Maestro himself. He thanked me for the book and also invited me to his home, since he was interested in meeting "the strange person who makes a gift of burned books." My scheme had worked.

The Maestro lived in the center of town, on the second floor of an old building. Beside the apartment door a bronze plaque identified the resident. I was ushered in by a heavy-set, middle-aged woman whose voice I immediately recognized: it was the same one that had issued the phone rejection. She seemed to be accustomed to people dropping in, since she asked me nothing. She led me into the living room, indicated an armchair, and left me. The room was simply furnished: several shelves filled with books, a few portraits hung over a large sideboard, and little more. On a small table lay the burned book. While I waited, I went to the window. The branches of a tree almost touched the glass and rose to the floor above. Outside there was a fairly large park but with only a few trees.

I was watching a teacher supervise her children's games in the park when I heard the sound of footsteps. I turned. It was the Maestro.

After a few words of introduction, we sat down before the window. The elderly man had taken up the Marlowe book and gave the impression that he was pleased to have it. With his warm encouragement, I dutifully related the circumstances of my acquiring it. Entertained by my account, the Maestro silently contemplated the book. Then, after a moment, he spoke.

"It's strange," he said, turning the book over in his hands. "But lately, with no apparent justification whatever, I have been trying to imagine what sort of suffocation I might feel, what stigmata might appear on my body if one of my books were condemned or thrown into a fire. I say this because I have no doubt that each book contains a particle of its author, a kind of captive genie to whom only a reader can provide some small relief. So consider the damage that could be inflicted on that imprisoned atom by condemnation or by fire. Damage, moreover, that might not be long in affecting the author himself, in the end a victim of something akin to a voodoo ritual. And now, suddenly, this book . . . I don't know, I don't know. But anyway, as you are aware, my work until now has been ignored by those dedicated to punishing writers, so I have no recourse but to continue imagining. It's odd . . . I was once on the verge of writing a story in which an Asian despot—or a South American one—instead of destroying a book, orders that the eyes of all possible readers be blinded and then that a copy be sent to each of them; I no longer recall why I didn't write it. But now, with regard to this book (and the old man stroked the volume as if offering it consolation), I must say that I would like very much to know its story. By that I mean I'd like to find out the cause of the fire that almost destroyed it, to know if it was premeditated or simply the result of a servant's carelessness; and know why it was not completely consumed and who saved it and who entrusted it to the indifference of a book seller. Besides, that a book whose pages describe a pact with the devil bears the signs of fire seems a little disconcerting, don't you think? Well, perhaps some day I'll decide to tell its history myself, in a story or a poem."

Having said this, he thanked me again for the gift. The warmth with which he was speaking and the gentle tone that his words at times took on quickly dissipated the (totally incomprehensible) tension that I had begun to feel as time passed and soon I found myself chatting enthusiastically with the writer. After some two hours, in spite of his apparent interest in continuing the conversation, I decided to leave, so as not to tire him out.

When he said good-bye, he told me he had definitely determined to write a poem on the subject of the book and that when it was finished I would be the first person to read it. He also called me "messenger of the Muses," or something similar.

Back home I happily considered that in a matter of a month or so I would have some news about the poem. But several months passed during which I had no word. One day I read in the paper that the writer had traveled abroad where he would remain for an extended period. His return was not announced anywhere, but the notice in a literary journal that a scheduled interview with the author had been postponed at the latter's request indicated to me that the Maestro was back in Buenos Aires. Nonetheless, the news of the delayed interview discouraged me from making any attempt to approach him. Resigned, I tried to put the whole matter out of my mind and returned to my customary duties.

Close to a month went by. One morning, when I was out, word came that the Maestro wanted to see me. I was pleasantly surprised by the message, and on the way to his apartment I reproached myself for certain thoughts I had had concerning his silence. In the end he had not forgotten his promise, and now he would surely show me his poem about the burned book. But what simple-mindedness on my part! Yes, it did turn out that he wanted to see me regarding a poem, but one whose subject and substance involved a concept so fantastic that what I was imagining at that moment was reduced to something laughable and infantile.

The Maestro himself opened the door. Almost a year had passed since our last meeting. I found him now looking a little older. He seemed preoccupied and a noticeable excitement, which he soon overcame, gave his body and his movements a deceptive sense of energy.

We sat down in the same place as the time before. Everything in the room was just as it had been on that occasion, which gave me the impression that scarcely a day had passed since then. At the outset the writer offered his apology for having remained out of touch, a circumstance that he assured me had been unavoidable; then, his gaze fixed on me in an inquisitive manner, he began questioning me about my activities. He asked about the makeup of my family, touched only briefly on the subject of literature (which, it seemed to me, he had no concern for whatever). The interest and the tone he displayed in the inquiries revealed to me that my presence, for reasons I could not discern, was important to him.

The examination continued for a while longer and by all indications I passed, since after a silence and more probing glances (which I pretended to ignore) he began to speak again.

"Yes," he said, alluding to certain comments I had made about the contrast between my ambitions and my present condition, "at times we must carry out duties that have no connection with our true intimate nature. But even when it comes to extremely important questions, scarcely any chosen person owes his condition as such to a suitable matching of character and mission. On the contrary, that one (or those) who does the choosing seems to take enjoyment from the impediments and unexpected results that stem from the inappropriate combining of . . . organ and function, to use the evolutionist's jargon. Take my case: do I appear to have what is necessary to be a chosen one, a hero? But be that as it may (and to get directly to our subject), let me say to you that your presence here is the result of my having been given the appearance of a hero, of a chosen one. If the designer of this plan had been permitted a personal consultation, there is no doubt that I would have been considered unworthy. You see, I have decided that you should be the only one to know of the secret that has been the reason for my success. But don't be alarmed. This all concerns a poem, as we understood at the time of our first meeting. It is, however, a poem that is very different from the one that you may have in mind. It is, of course, related to the book by Marlowe, but, to put it in one way, in a much more far-reaching sense. Broader and more extraordinary. Do you remember what I said at our first meeting, about how books contain some small particle of the author in them? Yes? Well, the Marlowe volume that you gave me had concealed within it something like that. In fact, something more than that: a key, a riddle (a devilish one, if you will) that set into motion a gigantic wheel, within whose spokes I now find myself entrapped, terrified and happy at the same time.

"But this all belongs to the story and I don't want to begin it without warning you that I am in no way able to offer you any concrete feature, any proof, that will bear out what I am going to tell you. I admit that I do possess such proofs, but you will soon realize why it is not advisable that I confide them to you—at least for the time being. Besides, I must confess that I have given much thought to the desirability of describing to you what is going on. And now if I have decided to do so, I am not entirely sure why. Possibly it may simply be the need to place some distance between myself and these events. And, too, since this all began with you and your book . . . I really don't know. Well, it is of no particular importance, so let us get to the story.

"As I have said, it all began with your book. As it happened, that day, after you left, I went to my study with the intention of writing down certain phrases that had stuck in my mind during our conversation and that were related to the idea of the poem about the book. But as soon as I sat down at my desk, I discovered that I didn't recall a single one of them, and this in spite of the fact that just moments before I had repeated them to myself out loud. To try to bring them back, I attempted writing something down. But even though I concentrated as much as I could on the subject, I could not produce a single thought or image. Attributing it to my weariness, I decided to abandon the effort until another occasion. A few nights later, I felt sufficiently clear-headed to try once more. It was futile; after repeated attempts, I could not get past the first verse, and it, in fact, was no better than mediocre. There was no sense in persisting. Weary and troubled, I went to bed.

"In spite of my age, I do not experience the problems associated with old age, such as rheumatism or gout, but the absence of these is compensated with a particularly aggravated case of insomnia, which has nothing to do with the lack of sleep common in older people, and which I have been afflicted with for some years now. That night was no exception. Waiting for sleep to overcome me, I began thinking, in vague terms, about the poem, which was threatening to turn into an obsession worse than any I had ever known. Images of fire, shouting voices, pages in the wind, scenes from ancient tragedies, symbols, crosses, and all sorts of visions raced through my mind. Little by little, they began to come together; then their shapes became vague and finally a gray, soporific mist settled over my consciousness. Immediately, a final shudder, a grateful *At last,* uttered or imagined, and suddenly nothingness.

"Then I dreamed the following: on a stormy night, like that of a fable, I was seated at my desk, trying to write a poem; but in spite of the effort I was putting into it, I could not produce one line. Even more than that, as if someone had placed a pen in the hand of a caveman, all I could do was fill the paper with lines and scrawls. At the same time, my senses had become so intensified that I could hear the beat of the rain on the terrace and, beyond this, see the birth of the lightning flashes. A cold sweat ran down my forehead, moistening the paper and the surface of the table. After a moment, the entire room—except the desk and myself—began to rotate slowly. I closed my eyes. When I opened them, the walls had acquired such a velocity that I found myself surrounded by a streaked and motionless curtain. I looked at the curtain as if I were a spectator waiting for it to rise and for the performance to begin. It did not go up, of course, but before me there emerged, slowly at first and then becoming clearer, a section of the bookcase. Briefly, I looked over the books, whose titles were legible at that distance. Then a feeling of weariness caused me to relax my gaze. Suddenly, I thought I noticed that one of the books had moved. Startled, I leaned forward and looked closer. Immediately, it moved once again until it stood out in relation to the other books. I tried to rise but I could not. With perfect ease I then reached out my arm—which had acquired sufficient length to reach clear to the shelf—and I removed the book. It was the one you had given me. I placed it on the desk—my arm had assumed its normal length—looked away and opened it at random; then still without looking, I began running my index finger over the page. Somewhere near the middle of the page my finger encountered something that seemed to be raised. I looked down; except for the paper and the printing on it, there was nothing. I read the line that my finger had stopped at. It was the beginning of the scene where Faust indicates to Mephistopheles the wishes and conditions that were to be communicated to Satan. But as I began to read over the lines of this invocation that were so well known to me, I noticed that the fragment had been modified. There, where Faust demands from the Infernal Powers so many years of voluptuous indulgences, this or that special ability, there appeared a request that, compared with the original, was nothing short of amazing. He was asking to be granted the capacity to create a poem whose verses would be, once and for all times, the essence and absolute model of poetry. Something, in effect, like the Poem of Poems. Curiously, I didn't give any importance to the apocryphal nature of the text, but instead stood up and recited it out loud as the desk again merged into the curtain that enclosed the room.

"The recitation ended when one of my fingers on the hand holding the book suddenly began to bleed. I held the hand out and let the drops of blood fall to the floor, where they formed a small but unsettled puddle, as if they were drops of quicksilver. When the bleeding stopped (I felt no pain in the finger nor did it show any kind of laceration), the little pool began to disintegrate, and from each of the fragments letters began to appear, which in turn formed words, so that in an instant the invocation was written on the floor in my own blood . . .

"I closed the book, prepared to recite the text laid out on the floor, when a deafening din shook the room and filled it with a blinding light that prevented me from seeing anything. Dazed and nearly blinded, I immediately felt that my head was growing monstrously in size and taking on the round and hollow shape of a cauldron, from the bottom of which there emerged a murmur that, once it had ceased growing, produced a roar of crashing waves that seemed more than the dimensions of my brain could contain. But shortly thereafter, as commonly occurs in dreams, my perception shifted to a different and not very clear perspective, one from which I could suddenly see myself appear, in the form of an archangel, hovering over what had once been my head. Following a few flutterings of orientation and coinciding with the repositioning there of all my faculties, that figure, my winged personification fearfully approached the center of the crater, from which point the cause of the deafening phenomenon became instantly clear: within that cauldron (the cauldron of my head!) were echoing all the words that all men had ever imagined and created, in all languages and dialects, dead or still in use. Millions of phonemes were blending there their timeless music to the arbitrary and madcap sounds that were produced here and there by the colliding together of the signs that represented them. Every now and then, when the buzz of that linguistic broth diminished a little, I was able to capture some words in languages known to me, which at times were entangled in grotesque unions (the word *luna,* for example, was combined with *mentecato, labyrinth* with *fusciarra, caelum* with *enclenque . . .*) or, in contrast, by miraculous coincidence and blending their rhythms (*arc-en-ciel* with *Nachtigall* with *amapola* with *tristezza . . .),* they combined into a selective garland of sounds that delivered to my ears the tranquility of their cadence, perfect and composed for the ages. Some sounds, moreover, stood out for their electric undulation and produced a noise similar to the hiss of a snake. I remember particularly a symmetrical and glistening *A* gripped by the thorny curvature of certain oriental characters; it remained for an instant on the surface, indecisively, and then sank back down together with its captors.

"In the meantime, the body that was sustaining that phenomenon had scarcely grown, and from above the archangel could hardly make out the arms that waved to it in farewell—or perhaps it would be more correct to say, that were calling for help. In any case, the feverish activity gradually ceased and finally the little arms became motionless. The body and the "thing" that crowned it continued there, unmoving, like a useless and forgotten object. The archangel perched on the edge of the cauldron, folded its wings and looked down into the interior. The signs had ended up flowing together and now formed a dark and serene lake, in whose surface the archangel was reflected. The latter remained quiet for a moment; then pushed off and dove into the lake. At that instant a bolt of lightning wakened me; through the window the first light of a new day was beginning to filter in. This is what I dreamed, or what, judiciously, I want to believe that I dreamed."

The Maestro paused. He seemed tired and he was breathing with difficulty, as if he had fought his way out of the dream he described.

Night had fallen. The servant appeared, dressed to leave, and turned on the lights. She directed a remark to the writer and left.

The Maestro went to the door and locked it. When he came back he disconnected the phone and went to the window and looked out on the street. The boisterous song of the sparrows, identical to that of the morning, filled the room.

"They are preparing to receive their sparrow dreams," he said, "and they do so with flattering songs so that their dreams don't turn into nightmares."

I agreed with a smile. At this point the Maestro sat down once more and proceeded with his account.

"Well, let's continue. That morning, as soon as I got up, I went to the bookshelf and took down the singed book. On the indicated page, the text that I found—the one that had been modified in the nightmare—was the one that Marlowe had written. This confirmation troubled me but at the same time, with some embarrassment I reproached myself for having doubted what I would find. But shortly afterward, I began to feel unaccountably disturbed. Also a certain enervation, alternating with periods of heightened stimulation previously unknown to me, was preventing me from carrying out any task whatever. Toward noon, noting that the sensation that had gripped me since the morning was increasing, I decided to cancel all appointments for that afternoon. I felt that I was anticipating 'something' whose nature I could not determine and that at the same time, little by little, though I tried to ignore it, the dream and the mood that accompanied it were beginning to crowd out any other thought. (The scene that most insistently returned to my memory was that of the incantation and within it the false text.)

"Some time later I went to the bookshelf, took down the damaged book and, with the idea in mind of dislodging the dreamed, apocryphal fragment, I recited Marlowe's verses several times out loud. But after each repetition the false text imposed itself on me with renewed vigor. I set the book aside without understanding what was happening.

"Certain details of that afternoon have been erased from my memory, but still I recall that at nightfall I found myself seated at my desk, trying to write. I recall, too, that I was trying to concentrate on the subject of the scorched book. But I could not; after several attempts I managed nothing more than a series of disconnected sentences and hackneyed images. The harder I tried, the harder the task became. And it was not just my mind but also my hand that was becoming paralyzed, just as it happened in the terrible dream. I gave up then any effort at writing and went to bed, now deeply disturbed.

"I will not go into unnecessary details of what occurred during the days following. Let it suffice to say that all my efforts to write, all my attempts at creation, failed miserably. The simplest subjects seemed beyond my reach. A child would have had an advantage over me. And the profoundly disturbing nature of those failures was intensified by the reappearance of what, in short, I will call the *sensation* (whose effect I have already described to you) that took over my entire being at the moment when I tried to write. At night, during the times when I was able to sleep, the dreams intensified. At first they were disconnected dreams; but later they were transformed into variations on the theme of the incantation, the memory of which, I swear to you, never left me during the day. So that the moment came when I was no longer sure if wakefulness existed or if it all was a continuous dream.

"It was precisely in that state of apparent sleepwalking, as the signs began accumulating about me, that I finally accepted the possibility that the influence of the dream could manifest itself in my waking life, and that the incantation, be it a product of my own most deeply repressed desire or the playful handiwork of some satanic Prometheus, could be realized within the limits of everyday existence. Nevertheless, in an effort to reduce the demoniacal aspect of the matter (actually, as a means of holding onto my reason) I took refuge in a single word of the incantation: *capacity*. I, that is to say, the text I dreamed, was requesting the *capacity* to compose a poem, not that it should appear magically. Viewed from this angle, the feat seemed somehow more attainable to me. But given all this, how to attain that ability? Impatiently, I undertook to create a 'context': I disconnected the phone, let correspondence accumulate, and even went so far as to let the servant go, having her come only once a week to do the shopping and clean the apartment. Astonishingly, as a result of my determination the nightmares ended and the very memory of the dream faded almost to the point of disappearing.

"I then went back to reading with my customary passion. That evening I returned to the study and tried to write something, since that was part of my plan. But once I faced a blank sheet of paper, I could not come up with a single verse. It was not even allowed to me to bring together three or four words in coherent order. I persisted in spite of everything and gave no thought to imposing a time limit for the undertaking. As time went on, however, and despite my interest, the effects of the isolation and the frustration were increasingly evident. I became upset for the slightest reason, could not tolerate any kind of noise and—most disturbing—I was uncomfortable reading or listening to music. It was reasonable to suppose that if things continued in this way my nervous system, already sensitized to the extreme, would suffer a collapse. Given this prospect, even though it might bring on a return of the nightmare, I decided to abandon my efforts and resume the normal routine of my life. I reconnected the telephone, welcomed my friends (all of them very intrigued) and scheduled an occasional interview. Invitations to travel came from abroad, some of which I accepted. The exposure to new cities, sometimes producing surprises and other times disappointments, cleansed my mind. When I returned home, the dream and the nightmares were nothing but a frightful memory. Even so, I decided to wait awhile before writing anything.

"One day, I went out for a walk around the area of the Recoleta cemetery. It was a beautiful fall afternoon. The ground cover displayed bright green and yellow shades and the sun, which had barely warmed the air, cast over people and objects a subtle gold aura that raised all that it touched to a heightened state of peace and grace. My mental outlook was excellent and I truly felt—why not admit it?—happy. I was strolling around outside the walls of the cemetery when, turning off onto Vicente López, the noisy chatter of a circle of six or seven dancing children caused me to stop and regard them with delight. The joyful mood of the group and the simple purity of their songs filled my heart with nostalgia and images of my childhood came quickly to mind. Almost without noticing it, I approached the children. One of the girls, the oldest, whom the rays of the sun had transformed into a Madonna, looked my way and began pulling her companions over to me. Then, amid song and laughter, they continued their dance in a circle around me. I stood in the middle, like a sort of ancient idol who is to be honored and from whom wondrous miracles are expected. The boisterous tone expanded and became increasingly contagious. Then there occurred something that still today astonishes and perplexes me. Time stopped. All sound and all movement stopped. The world, at least that piece of it, the circle of children, I myself, everything surrounding, acquired the stillness of a painting. It was as if, without warning, the Day of Judgment had arrived and all that was missing was for the dead to climb over the cemetery walls and announce the news. Suddenly, from the circle of children there arose an exquisitely sweet voice intoning (I'm not sure this is the right word) something that resembled a song, but in a way that was extraordinary, since abruptly and without modifying the volume or the tone, that voice split into a spectrum of identical voices, each of which uttered, without superimposing itself over the others, a single and separate word—in whose letters vibrated almost imperceptibly the melody of the song. This inconceivable occurrence preserved the overall harmony and produced at the same time a confusion of varying and vibrating—but compatible—sounds, into which I emerged, both lulled and fearful. Then, entranced by this series of sustained passages, on the point of losing consciousness over the voluptuous sensation, the effect and the tempo of the song began to diminish. Next there was a whirling of sounds and afterward a recapitulation, and then something astonishing in the midst of what was already miraculous: the voices of the disconnected chorus blended into the original voice, which intoned (this time I feel the term is exact) a stanza whose verses were made up of words belonging to the previous disorganized jumble. I don't know how to describe what happened from then on. I recall that the verses of the song flowed like a subtle breeze through my body and came to rest in my head, where my memory seized on each word the way a drowning man grasps at a timber, since I felt that if I didn't succeed in holding onto that wondrous thing, I was lost.

"But, aware of it or not, I had been preparing myself for months for such a moment, and neither my memory nor my body were going to fail to capture it. As the child finished her song, movement was restored and everything about me resumed its customary rhythm.

"I quickly left the children, walking a short distance to recover my composure. I closed my eyes then and repeated the verses out loud. My astonishment was beyond description: that simple stanza converted everything I knew about the concept of poetry into so much mindless nonsense, into an example of hackneyed handiwork that any poet conscious of his creative power and of the model that he aspires to would have disdainfully cast into the wastebasket. "Musicality" was not its main virtue, and yet every time that I uttered it I felt that its melodiousness would be capable of harmonizing and blending any opposing elements, elements apparently irreconcilable and destined to remain forever separated. Nor was its virtue what we call 'sense,' yet the wisdom and knowledge that it bestowed sufficed to refute our most cherished concepts, reducing them to fruitless speculations. And these two qualities seemed to be imbued with a most unusual sensation (of which I told you I had had a foreshadowing, remember?), or, perhaps more precisely, they communicated that sensation by means of the mood that the verses created as they were recited, a mood comparable to that evoked by a cistern in which exotic flowers are decomposing, or to the aroma of a cemetery after a rainfall, a mood whose most specific effect consisted of a sense of weakness that debilitated my being and caused my will to falter as if it were under the spell of a sorcerer. Almost immediately, I made another discovery: with the repetition of the lines my mouth seemed to become filled with burning embers, since the sweet, fragile covering that each word was encased in fell away with the first savorings, revealing their true nature, their essential identity. And most astonishing was the fact that they were common words, simple words, known to you and me, but that—it is important to stress this—like the ingredients of an explosive formula, acquire their devastating force only on being brought together.

"As you will have comprehended, the verses spoken by the girl belonged to the Poem. The Poem of the incantation, of course. So long a wait, so many thoughts about its appearance—which were still with me up to the moment before—and then suddenly this magical eruption that delivers to my ears one of its sections. How could there be any mistake, any doubt? At the same time, on recovering from the emotion and wanting to keep this treasure to myself, I looked around cautiously at my surroundings; there was no one nearby. The sun had now set and the children had been replaced by two drunks who were preparing to spend the night at the foot of the wall. I took a taxi and returned home.

"Once there I ran to the study and, trembling, wrote out the stanza, the verses at last revealed to me, with the delicacy of a monk illuminating a manuscript. The sheet of paper, I swear to you, grew warm at the touch. Now, greatly encouraged, I tried to complete the Poem then and there. But once more I was overwhelmed by the familiar sense of the impossibility of writing and by a sudden and unpleasant indisposition that obliged me to leave the studio and lie down for a while.

"In bed, I was gripped by a strange anxiety, a kind of sorrowful regret. Because that instant of revelation and reaction had put an end to the rule of calculation and probability, of fiction, and turned the explorer of the marvelous *on paper,* the delver into the possibilities of magic, into the docile object of an unfathomable fiction, of a deadly serious game whose rules certainly do not admit the possibility of a dissociation. But this lasted only a few minutes. Precisely, until I recited the verses once again. In their presence, my scruples and my fears quickly dissolved and that night I slept sustained by the great joy I felt as the possessor of a part of the Poem."

The Maestro fell silent.

His face had undergone a transformation as the narrative unraveled and, on reaching this point, it had the rigid and stark appearance of a death mask. His voice seemed to be emerging from a deep well, although it was clear and resonant. Suddenly he stood up, took a few steps, and picked up a photograph and handed it to me. It was of him, but at an earlier age. When I returned it, without having understood his intention, he explained:

"It was taken three months ago."

For the first time since he had begun to tell his story, I sensed anguish in his voice.

He asked me if he could turn out the lights, and I assented. He switched them off and the room was dappled with the moonlight that filtered in through the tree next to the window. Then he sat down with the photograph in his hands and continued speaking.

"From that day on my health deteriorated rapidly. It was obvious that together with the gift came a corresponding penalty, a price imposed on the revelation that I did not want to dwell on. Something disturbed me: the urgency of knowing how the rest of the Poem would be revealed to me. I understood that my efforts to force its appearance had been rejected. It was necessary to forget it (or to pretend to forget it), to display a humble attitude, one of resignation, for it to appear. But now would that approach be enough to complete the revelation? Or would a more aggressive attitude on my part be necessary? And in that case, what kind of action? How long would I have to wait? . . . In the end, I said to myself: a dream in which I read—in which I am *made to read*—the invocation of an ancient doctor, composed by an illustrious poet and into which I furtively inject my deepest desire, could this be realized at any given moment, as if it were a question of some sort of nursery riddle? Evidently, no. I could not manage it, and Someone did not wish it. For some reason only a part of it had been revealed to me. So then? So all I had to deal with was conjectures. For example, and rejecting a repetition of the previous *mise en scène* (magic is seldom overgenerous), the possibility that the most common circumstance or the most ordinary person would bring me close to the answer, or at least to a glimpse of it. I also imagined that most probably neither the verses nor the words would appear in their corresponding order, as in the first instance, a possibility that, I can assure you, did not trouble me. On the contrary, if it caused me to feel anything, it was contentment, since in this way my capacity for versification, curiously ignored until now, would at last be called upon . . .

"As you will note, each one of these conjectures was in fact a wish. And we know what happens to wishes: they are granted. Yes, just as I had foreseen, the fifth and sixth verses appeared in a less spectacular fashion. One afternoon, as I was rereading a work by Shakespeare (that there is no need to identify), I observed in certain words something out of proportion, in a sense inappropriate or excessive. Such is not uncommon in this author, but the curious thing was that they appeared in passages wherein the choice of words had always impressed me. Alerted, I wrote down the words (there must have been fifteen or twenty of them) and I began to compose verses. At the start, and until I determined that I had recovered my ability to weigh the value of words and write poetry, I used only a few of them. But since in the first attempt I succeeded in producing two or three lines that seemed tolerable, with one of these especially good, I immediately decided to take the leap and use nothing but Shakespeare's words. First, in a playful mood, I composed two verses that signified nothing, but whose comical incongruity helped me to relax a bit more. Then, in a more serious attempt, I shuffled the words into a vertical list, then a diagonal one, then in a horizontal line. The latter effort produced a few expressions that took on a strange emphasis, a certain phosphorescence. Setting them aside, I then jumbled the remaining words together, combining them first in one way and then another. I played with prefixes, I constructed anagrams, and slowly the glow of the first words was extended to the others. In the end, I succeeded in constructing two lines that, at first sight (actually it was a matter of *sensation*), convinced me that I was in the presence of the true verses. These same lines, out of place because of the requirements of the Poem, appeared withered, drained, possessing only their habitual meanings. The word 'tree' *sounds* and *tells* us the same in a poem as in a botanical treatise. Here, however, having found its 'prescribed' place, each word recovered its primitive condition, its light and its cosmos.

"The new verses exhibited the same perfection as the earlier ones and achieved the same impact. They seemed to come from some dimension where opposites do not exist, since through my contact with them I felt that my sensations and my perceptions were united. My hand, in the presence of this stimulus, was identical with my brain and it understood as much.

"I immediately fell ill. After consultations and analyses (all of this undertaken at the urging of my friends), I was diagnosed as having had a nervous breakdown, the result of overwork. Realizing that they were useless, I pretended to comply with the medical requirements. By then I was convinced that nothing would happen to me until I fulfilled the terms of the dream. Nevertheless, and quite fortunately, my ability to identify the words and compose the verses increased over that period. Discovering them, in fact, soon became almost a game, since from a certain moment on, as if I had developed my own radar, there began to function something in my brain like a sound wave system that informed me when I confronted the phonic character of a word—if it was the appropriate one—because the sound would acquire a marked dissonance. As for my vision, it, too, possessed a similar capacity; in this case, consisting of a kind of corrosive substance capable of penetrating the outer veneer that had accumulated on each word through custom and usage. If it was *the* word, it lit up before me as if touched by a flaming rod—although I should clarify that the important thing (a dictionary would have simplified the question) wasn't so much the words as the situation or the occasion in which I encountered them. Thus I could see or hear a certain word many times in a day, but only at *that* moment did it seem different.

"Altogether I had managed to assemble seven verses when there occurred a pause of some five months . . . a terrible time whose details I prefer to keep to myself. What I will tell you is that although my health and appearance notably improved, it took only a week, during which I was able to compose a new line, for me to return to a state even more deplorable than the previous one.

"The following verses were created in a month. Between the tenth and eleventh, a fortnight passed. Surprisingly, perhaps in a way associated with the well-known euphoria of the dying man, my health improved with the two latest verses. Even so, facing each new day brings forth in me the same state of exhaustion that years before it took some two months of labor to reach.

Fortunately, certain unmistakable signs now indicate to me that the end is near."

The old man stopped talking.

Freed by the darkness of the obligation of looking into his face as he told his story, I had remained for almost all of the last portion with my head in my hands. Only when he finished talking did I change my position slightly and look into his face. The impression that I got was such that my hands involuntarily moved forward in a gesture of rejection. The writer's face had lost its previous rigidity and it now seemed that the mask, as if melting, was beginning to distribute down and to the sides the thick putty-like mass of his shapeless features, which, a moment later when the movement ceased, acquired a stony, cracked appearance. Only his eyes seemed to escape this solidification that turned the Maestro into a mummy, and like two dark spiders they continued their rapid movement between the narrowed slits of his eyelids.

I was horrified. I felt suddenly nauseated and a tingling sensation spread through my legs. All of the tension produced by the narrative, which I had taken pains to conceal behind an expression of relaxed interest, was released at the sight of that Sphinx. I felt I had to turn on the light, call out to someone or get up and run out, but some unknown force held me in place. Fortunately, the Sphinx turned toward the window and his features, seen in profile, were not so disturbing, but rather now seemed comical, like a Greek mask. Suddenly, in a soft voice, he began to sing a song in English. This act, so human and unexpected, calmed me down somewhat and slowly, while the impact of the previous shock gradually lessened, I began looking around the room we were in, pursuing the fleeting thought that the Poem should be lying about, on a table somewhere, phosphorescent and contagious. But I saw nothing out of the ordinary.

In the meantime, the murmur coming from the Maestro continued. In order to dispel the sensation that persisted within me I began walking around the room, idly examining one object or another. From time to time the Maestro gave a side glance in my direction, but without seeming to have become aware of my extreme reaction to his metamorphosis. Abruptly, he stopped singing. I turned slightly: the Maestro had risen to his feet and was looking out the window. I had the impression that he was talking to himself, taking no note of my presence. Uncomfortable now, I turned on the light.

As the light filled the room, the Maestro turned in surprise. I, too, was surprised: his appearance was now the same as when he received me. Only the traces of a profound weariness now marked his features. I sighed in relief and happily smiled at the old man as if I had just run into him unexpectedly. I considered then (perhaps too frivolously) that the startling previous effect must have been produced by a particular play of light and shadow that the moon and the trees had projected into the room, augmented by the suggestive nature of his story. I apologized to him for the light, explaining that I wanted to see the time on my watch. "It's almost midnight," he murmured; then he added: "My day is beginning."

The latter observation he uttered in an ambiguous tone that suggested uneasiness and resignation at the same time, so that it could be interpreted as a reflection on the imminent insomnia or also as a foreshadowing of the definitive nature of the new day.

He sat down again and gestured to me to do the same; but I chose to remain standing. He offered me something to drink, but I declined. Still uneasy, I could think of nothing else but getting away from there so that I could calmly reconsider all that had happened. It was evident (the Maestro's attitude confirmed it) that with regard to his story there was nothing more to add. The final outcome, unforeseeable or perhaps admitting some conjecture, could be a long time in the coming, despite the writer's hopes. Besides, there was the matter of preserving the proofs . . .

Several minutes passed in silence. I was struck by the Maestro's lack of interest in knowing my opinion of his story. I thought, too, that possibly he was feeling some regret over having confided it to me. When he spoke again, however, he advised me to let a few days go by and then, with some perspective, try to analyze his story and the consequences that could result from such a fantastic occurrence. He apologized once more for having turned me into his "accomplice" and—half seriously, half in jest—implored me not to react to his account the way that any of his friends would have: considering it as "just one more hoax from the Old Man, who wants so much to play the mystagogue that he doesn't hesitate to insert his fantasies into reality or compromise real persons in order to infuse life into his creations." I said that I wouldn't and in turn urged him not to fail to let me know when his Poem was completed.

He was smiling when I left him.

Ten years of insomnia, it is told, were accumulated by the slave entrusted by Clitemnestra to await the signal that would announce the fall of Troy, a period that lasted up until his vigil was illuminated by the fire set on top of a hill. That night, when I left the Maestro's home, I feared that I might be subjected to the rigors of a similar wait, and I resolved that, unlike the last time I left him, my enthusiasm with respect to his promise would be moderated. Besides, before it was about a poem; now, on the other hand . . . I did not put the matter out of my mind entirely, but rather, overcoming certain inhibitions, I began to prepare an outline of this story, for which I planned to invent a provisional ending, until the time when I learned the true one. But a few nights later, with only two or three pages written down, the phone rang. It was the Maestro. He seemed excited and his voice sounded muffled. Nonetheless, I understood he was telling me *Come, come,* and once or twice, *It's fantastic.* I don't know if he heard my voice, because the words I spoke were answered by the sound of the receiver being replaced at his end. I was greatly surprised; I had already considered the possibility that he would not call me again. For that reason, on hearing his voice, all sorts of ideas and sensations crowded into my head, although the emotion of the moment prevented me from focusing on anything more than the Maestro's face and the title of the Poem, which, I have forgotten to mention, he had decided to call simply *The Poem.* Beneath these words, I could only intuit something resembling a cluster of flames.

I went quickly down to the street and took a taxi. During the ride I imagined the Maestro in a pitched battle with "something" terrible, a kind of Dragon-Poem of extraordinary ferocity.

When I got out of the taxi, I noticed that there was a light in his window. The street door stood partly open. I went up to his apartment and rang the bell two or three times. As I waited, I looked at my watch; it was almost midnight. Impatiently, I rang the doorbell again, a long ring; no one answered. I was becoming worried. To determine if anyone was inside, I looked through the keyhole of the door; the key had been inserted in the other side. I thought about notifying the *portero* but the certainty that something important was in the offing made me reject the idea; I had to get in one way or another. To be sure, I waited for a moment and rang the bell again: nothing.

Then I made up my mind. I pulled out several pages of the newspaper that was lying outside the apartment's service door and pushed them most of the way under the door; then I poked at the key in the lock with my pen-knife until it fell onto the paper, which I then pulled out carefully so that the key would not fall off. I opened the door trembling and advanced a few steps. There was no one in sight. I called out but there was no response. The door to the study stood part way open and there was a light on inside. I approached slowly, pushed open the door and, fearing the worst, entered the study. I was not mistaken; there was the Maestro in his chair, bent over the desk, his head resting on his left arm; his right hand held a pen. He looked as if he had fallen asleep. I touched him gently; his right hand fell to one side and the pen rolled off the desk onto the floor; he was dead.

Instinctively, as a sudden concern crossed my mind, I stepped back, but the reigning silence erased the fear of anything strange or out of place. On the desk were several books, among them the Marlowe volume. Under the dead man's left hand, half hidden, was a crumpled sheet of paper, on which he had apparently been writing before he died. Compelled by the sight of that sheet, I stepped forward and tried to move the hand. The instant I did so, I shrank back as if a snake had bitten me: the Maestro's hand was as hot as fire! I was horrified by the contact with that burning flesh and for a moment I didn't know what to do. Finally, I took a book and my handkerchief and, setting the book on the edge of the paper that the hand clenched, I tried to separate the fingers, protecting my own hand with the handkerchief. With some effort I was able to loosen them slightly and could then make out part of what was written there: *The Poe* . . . Seeing that title and wanting to heighten the moment of discovery, I closed my eyes. Then, very slowly, I moved the sheet away from the Maestro's fingers. The paper seemed to crackle at the touch.

Only when I had freed the sheet did I open my eyes and look at it. At first glance, I could see nothing but flashing words, since my excitement was so great that I was looking without seeing, my vision blurred. I took a deep breath and prepared to read more calmly. Yet when I looked at the first word of the first verse, something so extraordinary occurred that still now when I recall it, my knees get weak. I observed with true horror that as my eyes ran over the verse it disappeared, it faded from sight so that I could not read anything. I tried to start reading at the end of each line, but the movement of my eyes across the paper left only an ashen trail. I looked at the last word of the Poem: it disappeared at the first instant that my gaze fell on it, making it impossible for me to identify it. I closed my eyes for a few seconds. When I opened them and tried to read the words, which remained visible if I didn't look at them directly, they started to disappear. Before the entire poem disappeared, I threw the sheet on the desk and, sensing that I was the victim of the most ghoulish hallucination, on the very verge of fainting, I collapsed into a chair. I struck myself in the face and rubbed my eyes, trying to awaken from what seemed a nightmare. But I was wide awake and certainly this was not explained away as some sort of dream or optical illusion, since I could read any other text without difficulty, as I determined by glancing at one of the books on the desk.

After a few minutes, I picked up the sheet again. There remained a few words, scattered here and there, ready to fade into nothingness the moment I tried to read them. Then, in an angry impulse of perverse stubbornness, I fixed my gaze on each one of them until nothing remained on the paper but a few smudged black lines. Then I knelt next to the Maestro and began to weep softly, while the useless sheet of paper, like a white flame, seemed to sizzle in the fingers of my hand that was clutching it.

Translated by D.A.Y.